THE MENDICANTS

OF

LONDON.

u

A ROMANCE OF REAL LIFE.

BY ONE WHO HAS CARRIED A WALLET.

"The Mendicants of London are the best actors in the world."—MAXWELL.

"The facility with which unthinking kindness is imposed on, and the fair prospect of obtaining at no very great risk, and with the pleasurable excitement which attends a somewhat hazardous pursuit, a jovial living, keep up a standing corps of plunderers, and tempt into their ranks a constant succession of recruits."—The TIMES, Jan. 4, 1849.

LONDON:

A. VICKERS, 5, HOLYWELL STREET, STRAND;

AND ALL BOOKSELLERS.

1849.

LONDON:
JAMES STEWARD, PRINTER,
HARFORD PLACE, DRURY LANE.

THE
MENDICANTS OF LONDON.

" The Mendicants of London are the best actors in the world."   MAXWELL.

" We retrench the superfluities of mankind. The world is avaricious, and we hate avarice. A covetous fellow, like a jackdaw, steals what he was never made to enjoy, for the sake of hiding it. These are the robbers of mankind; for money was made for the free-hearted and generous: and where is the injury of taking from another what he hath not the heart to make use of?"

       GAY.

" With the ready trick and fable,
   Round we wander all the day;
And at night, in barn or stable,
   Hug our doxies on the hay.

What is title—what is treasure—
   What is reputation's care?
If we lead a life of pleasure,
   'Tis no matter why or where!

Life is all a variorum,
   We regard not how it goes;
Let them cant about decorum,
   Who have characters to lose.

Here's to budgets, bags, and wallets!
   Here's to all the wand'ring train!
Here's our ragged brats and callets!
   One and all cry out—Amen!"

       BURNS.

CHAPTER I.

THE MISER AND SPENDTHRIFT—REVENGE—A BRIDEGROOM AND WIDOWER IN A DAY.

AMONG the crowds of pedestrians which daily throng the busy streets of London, a solitary individual would pass along without attracting the notice of any one unless the detective eye of a mendicant selected him as a suitable person from whom to solicit alms.

One dark, foggy morning in the early part of November, as the large fingers on the various dials pointed to eleven, a light and slender figure, neatly attired, emerged from one of the narrow thoroughfares leading into Cheapside, and directed her course towards Cripplegate. She appeared to be about twenty years of age, and, from the simple elegance of her dress, to belong to the middle ranks of society.

As she entered Cheapside a poor emaciated female with a sickly child on each arm solicited a gratuity. The fair traveller, however, passed onwards, murmuring as she did so, " I dare say those were both borrowed children. But even if they were not hired for the purpose of imposition, I have nothing to give—nothing," she repeated, heaving a deep sigh.

The young girl proceeded onwards. In her route she passed a hale and robust old man, with bare head and healthy features, who was guided through the streets by a faithful dog, which carried in its mouth a small basket for the offerings of the benevolent.

Still our fair pedestrian passed onwards, without noticing the doleful accents of the old man.

" Pity the poor blind! For God's sake pity the blind!" repeated he at every step.

" I wonder if he really is deprived of sight? (murmured the young girl.) Perhaps it is that hypocritical Done, after all, and he only feigns blindness! But, alas! I have nothing to give," she repeated.

About the middle of the next street the young girl passed a wretched-looking heap of humanity, closely coiled up against the wall, with scarcely rags enough to cover him. He had traced with chalk in fair round characters on the pavement,—

     " I ham Starvin."

" Starving, no doubt, poor fellow (muttered the young girl), for the rags you have on are scanty enough; but as to food, alas! I question if you are in greater want than I am."

Onwards—still onwards, she journeyed, too

much absorbed in her own thoughts and proceedings to notice the numerous appeals to her charitable feelings that were from time to time tendered. She passed down the most deserted streets, with the view to escape observation as much as possible, and finally arrived opposite the church of the " Cripples Gate."

A considerable number of persons, among whom a small body of mendicants were conspicuous, had already assembled around the church.

At the period of which we write, the present laws against vagrancy were not in force, and, consequently, the mendicants now gathered before the church door were not prevented from assembling there.

The more respectable portion of those present gathered themselves into little groups of three and four each, the better to discuss the grand object for which they were assembled.

The mendicants, on the other hand, became isolated, or at least separated from their more fortunate neighbours; and, consequently, united themselves into a small coterie of the most grotesque description. There were mendicants of every kind, form, and character—beggars from necessity, and beggars by choice—persons afflicted, or apparently afflicted, with every infirmity common to human nature. There were blind, maimed, and deformed; young and old, pretty and hideous,—who came in heterogeneous order and joined the group.

The church of St. Sim...t in Cripplegate, or, rather, Cripples'-gate*, was a venerable building, and, unlike the present structure of that name, was protected by a strong iron railing.

Near the gate opening upon the passage which led to the church door, stood the band of mendicants alluded to. There were four or five of those choice spirits, who not only exhibited a perfect contrast to their companions, and most of the leading characteristics of the mendicants, but, being destined hereafter to figure somewhat conspicuously in these pages, are entitled to a more detailed description than the others.

In the middle of that group was an elderly man, taller, and, consequently, more conspicuous than the others, exhibiting a lofty forehead, surrounded by two tufts of grey hair; a meagre face, covered with dust; a large twisted nose and wide mouth, high fleshless cheek-bones, blood-shot eyes, with a brutal and ferocious expression. He seemed the living personification of those numerous figures placed in churches as the representation of Satan. He seemed maimed, and during the day exhibited a red patch on his right arm, which appeared to be

* So called from its being the spot where the cripples and mendicants of London usually assembled.

deprived of the hand. In that feature was embodied the abstract essence of the frightful personage—of an individual with strong passions determined to make use of them—a man who would not pause at anything, not even robbery and murder ! In short, it was the devil turned mendicant. This repulsive mien gave him the soubriquet of Black Bob.

Near his side might be seen a young girl, scarcely eighteen years of age. A handkerchief, and a garment without either form or colour, composed her " beggarly" attire. But the natural freshness and juvenile grace of the young girl, shone through her miserable clothing; although somewhat stained with dust, yet her fine and beautiful features were clearly perceptible through that partial obscurity. Her fine black sparkling eyes shone with a rich and natural brilliancy; her cheeks, of a graceful plumpness, exhibited a lively carnation truly enchanting, and her rosy mouth smiled with a simple gaiety. The doubtful nature of her dress, tumbled and stuck together as it was, only the better exhibited the exquisite proportions of her light round form. A vivacious cheerfulness and an earnest desire for pleasure on any terms, were clearly indicated in the expressive features of that charming creature.

Nearly opposite the latter, negligently supported on his crutches, was a mendicant about thirty years of age, apparently blind with one eye, and having a wooden leg. A partly bald head increased tenfold his large forehead, already furrowed with wrinkles; a large black bandage covered the sightless eye, but the other proved itself sufficiently ardent, lively, and expressive for both ; a vacancy of look, added to a bitter smile passing over his nerveless lips, without any apparent cause, and an air of continual abstraction, gave to his physiognomy, a mysterious and visionary appearance. Paying no attention to the significant oglings of the pretty mendicant before him, he uttered in an under-tone the words of a brief prayer.

The next figure of that group was a pious little old woman, attired in an ample black gown. The contour of her face was not yet deformed. The delicacy of her features and the fineness of her skin, now covered by the palor of age, as also an air of suffering, which enveloped her person, gave an impress of distinction foreign to her class. The shadow of the old black lace which decorated her cap and fluttered in the breeze, passed like a cloud of sadness over her inclined figure. She held in her hand a capacious bag, in which she deposited the gratuities presented to her. Although not very far advanced in age, yet she appeared afflicted with that nervous debility peculiar to the old and infirm.

About two steps from the old woman, and on the other side of the tall lame man, was a fat dumpling of a mendicant, crippled, maimed, and undoubtedly deprived of the use of his limbs; with the stumps of his legs supported by twenty pieces of wood, and progressing in a sort of timber-work frame which sustained him on every side. On his round plump face and brawny hands were depicted the evidences of rude health; his voice was full and mellow, and frequently betrayed the hearty jovial disposition with which he had been endowed. But these blessings were rather disadvantageous to him as a mendicant, because he thereby failed in creating that pity and compassion which were the objects of his life to secure; so much so, indeed, that he was frequently obliged to ask the assistance of his comrades, who, in a moment of happy humour, had bestowed upon him the nickname of Timbers.

Finally, beyond these, a middle-aged man might be seen standing, or rather leaning, alone against the iron railings of the church. The outline of his features, though extremely dark and lowering, was undoubtedly handsome, as far at it could be seen. A fine mouth and Roman nose were illuminated by two piercing eyes, fringed with the darkest lashes, and bordered by a pair of jet-black whiskers. His expressive countenance, prematurely furrowed by suffering and the exercise of strong passions, pourtrayed the secret workings of a vindictive spirit. He was attired in a complete suit of faded black, and wore an old fur cap, with which he enveloped his head, ears, and brow. A large neckerchief covered the lower part of his face in a manner which rendered it impossible for any one but his immediate companions to recognise him. He held in his hand a thick cane, divided in the middle by a brass joint, which he examined from time to time with an anxious and disturbed air.

"Look out there, look out!" cried the wooden-legged one-eyed visionary, with a proud and disdainful air; "the wedding is coming."

"It aint likely, my worthy Autumn * (said an old woman who came hobbling forward); there's no danger so long as the doors is shut an' yer brother isn't come; so you may make yerself aisy."

"Autumn aint such a fool as to trouble hisself about it without reason," added the fat Timbers from the middle of his scaffolding; "he would fain make us all retreat, in order to get a good place in front."

"Oh, as to the matter of that (observed another

* Autumn, in the vocabulary of the mendicants, signifies a preacher, or a church.

of the group), Autumn knows of other means of drawing tin to his pocket."

"And what are they, pray?" he demanded in a surly tone.

"I shan't say any arm of 'em (replied the mendicant); although they may be summut less christianlike than asking charity."

"Come, come, mother Merrymouth, (rejoined Autumn;) I am surprised that you, who still believe in witchcraft——"

"And if you have no faith in it, (interrupted she who had been addressed by so humorous an appellation,) why do you roost at the house of a fortinteller, who is supposed to have dealings with —— no matter?"

"What nonsense, you silly creature!"

"Come, come, peace!" cried Timbers; then continuing his conversation with Jenny's mother, and taking the pretty little mendicant by the hand, he jocularly added, "do you not notice how your daughter Jenny fattens, Mrs. Malpas? She gets stouter every day without knowing it, and will soon be as plump as myself, and that would be a pity."

"Do not mention it, pray (replied Mrs. Malpas); I tell her so every day."

"She is as fresh and blooming as the May rose," rejoined the crippled gallant.

"A fine figure to excite pity, truly! When she goes begging at the houses of the pious and charitable, she will obtain nothing with such a face. It is absurd to get so fat!"

"Nevertheless I only eat when I am hungry," observed Jenny, smiling good-humouredly.

"But you are so often hungry; and then you drink like a fish!"

"Ah, (exclaimed Timbers, with admiration,) but she is perfectly enchanting with a extra can; and so droll when she has had a little too much, that it's quite excusable."

"When a child, (resumed Mrs. Malpas,) she was thin and slender as she ought to be; and then, when I sent her to sing in the public streets, she got on capitally."

"So I do now when I go singing in the squares and respectable places (interrupted Jenny). Don't I get plenty of ribbon (money), and the notice of the gentry coves?"

"Notice! yes, no doubt. But you had better be careful on that score."

"Oh, ay! (resumed Jenny, humming a favourite air;) but isn't it delightful to sing one's own tune of 'Here's to the free-born maunder!' (mendicant)."

"Be quiet, Jenny."

"Pray bestow a trifle upon a poor cripple, my

good lady," said Timbers, addressing in a doleful tone the young girl whom we have previously seen hurrying hither. Then, as she passed him without response in her endeavour to reach the iron gate, he muttered in an under tone, "By jingo! but I think I have seen you before, madam. Give us a pinch of snuff, Mrs. Malpas. Between you and me, I must confess that Jenny's little slender figure would answer her purpose much better for mumping (begging) than such good looks; but she pleases me best as she is; in fact, she quite enchants me; will you give her to me in autumn (marriage), Mrs. Malpas? Will you have me, pretty Jenny?"

"No! the 'May-rose' wouldn't flourish if smothered by 'timber.' Besides, I love another," added the young girl, twinkling her eyes in the direction of Autumn, who did not notice her.

"As a marriage portion, (resumed the fat fellow, jocosely,) I would bring you my crutches and frame, which of themselves are sufficient to set you up as a match-maker; and I would add, hope——"

"Hope! (interrupted Jenny), did you say hope? That is droll coming from you, Timbers; for your life points towards the cemetery, whither you would lead me."

"Everybody goes there, sooner or later, Jenny; but it isn't every one as knows how to enjoy himself on the road. It's the artful dodger only that creeps into the public house on his way, and secures to himself the pleasures of life in its fleeting course."

"Ah, well, (resumed the young girl,) I don't wish to travel that way just yet, and though you appear so jovial and happy now, it cannot be long afore you are on that gloomy road, old boy."

Suddenly great movement was visible in the group, and each endeavoured to ascertain its cause. Autumn perceived the feeble Mary (whom we have already introduced to the reader, as the little old woman in black), rudely jostled by the other mendicants.

"Have a little care for poor Mary," he exclaimed in a sympathising tone, and making use of his crutch as a watchman uses his staff; "You'll knock the old woman down."

"Oh, aye! to be sure, (cried several voices,) a place in front for my lady there, in order that she may be able to grab all!"

"No, no, (replied the old woman,) you know that a little deserted corner suits me best."

"But yo are weak, Mary (insisted Autumn, compassionately); and this rough usage it's too bad."

"Never mind me; 'tis the trembling in my limbs that affects me most. I'll get into yonder corner and sit upon the steps," she added, retiring to the spot indicated.

A little fellow named Smasher, who had hitherto lived among the mendicants, ran towards the old woman, and with affectionate solicitude for her comfort, placed his thick greasy cap upon the stone. "There, (said he, pointing to the cap,) sit down on that granny, an' ye won't catch cold."

Then the lad, whose attention was immediately afterwards attracted to a distant part of the court, began to clap his hands, and laughed loudly, saying, "How they are shovin yonder! I must go an' see vot's up."

But it was more difficult to approach the scene of action than he had anticipated. Finding it impossible to make way through the crowd, he climbed over the railings into the church-yard, and thus obtained a good position to witness the fray.

The excitement had been caused by the attempt of a crooked, bandy-legged negro to secure for himself a good position for begging; but the mendicants, like the Americans, not acknowledging an equality of races, had raised against the poor black their sticks and crutches.

"Down with the imperdent Cæsar (cried they). Down with the willanous pagan, who carries on his face the devil's livery! Out with him. Get back to thy master's fire, ye imp of imperdence!"

The negro bounded like a top at each blow of his persecutors. The poor fellow had nearly lost the use of one side from head to foot, by a severe fall, in consequence of inattention to it at the time it occurred. His left arm, which had been broken in two or three places, had grown round, and his leg, taking the same course, did not touch the ground, except when required to walk, or rather hobble about. Nevertheless he was as agile, lively, and mischievous as if nothing were the matter with him.

Repulsed from one spot, he turned rapidly to another; driven from the front he attempted to escalade the iron railings at the side, but was again put to flight in a manner which excited the risibility of the whole fraternity.

In the meantime, many persons who were strangers to the proceedings, but attracted by curiosity, entered the assembled throng. Among that number, was a man of forty or forty-five years of age, rather decently attired, and holding in his hand a small pocket memorandum book. He was observed by the troop of mendicants, to whom, in fact, he belonged, though in a somewhat more elevated degree, as will be seen hereafter.

"Ah, Mr. Scrieve [cant term for begging letter writer,] good morning," they cried, as he forced his way through the group. "Ah, he takes no notice on us, 'cause he's better togs on his back than ve, and goes begging by strips (letters). Never mind the old 'poster, ve'll be even vith him some day. He's come to see who gives the most, so that he may write his long yarn to 'em. Ah, he's gone to plague poor Muffle, who seems dyin with the megrums."

The last observation referred to the dark personage with the remarkable cane.

" Old goose-quill will find lots of ribbon-folks here to-day," observed an old cripple.

"It's likely to be a splendacious marriage, is it, then?" said a poor woman, seizing the opportunity for inquiry.

"I believe ye," replied another voice.

The noise and chattering had now become general throughout the entire crowd, and one little coterie, composed of persons respectably attired, were extremely energetic in their discussion of the subject.

"It'll be a splendid affair, I suppose?" observed an old woman of the group.

"You're mistaken there, (replied a snuffling voice near her,) leastways for such grand folks."

"You know them, then?"

"I know the lady (save the mark!) an' her father a great deal too well," replied the voice.

"How so?"

"'Cos my husband, who was fool enough to go to law, got old Gripe to do his bisniss, an' was ruined in consequence. It's this way the old lawyer got his money."

"He's very rich, isn't he?"

"O, yes! Old Gripe's scraped up millions, they say, an' hoards it like a regular miser as he is. I've been two or three times to beg a little assistance from his daughter that's going to be married to-day, but she's as stingy as her old father, an' that's why I think it'll be a mean show after all."

"But the gentleman is young, noble, handsome, and generous, I have heard," observed a younger member of the party with a smile.

"Ay, that he is (replied another.) Viscount Vernon is as liberal as he is handsome; but, poor fellow, his father's been such a reckless spendthrift, that he is obliged to sell himself to old Gripe for gold, and comes here to hide his shame."

"Ha! ha! ha!" exclaimed a little old man, laughing heartily as he heard these remarks; "a fine match, truly! an excellent piece of business, indeed! It is a beautiful mercantile transaction, and admirably arranged, I must confess. One brings into the market a fine old name of ancient splendour, to which the other adds an immense capital, of equal importance in these days of speculation. It is a most delicious union, certainly!"

"They are coming! they are coming!" said several voices at the extremity of the street.

A general movement in the crowd proved that the announcement was not premature. The church doors were immediately thrown open, and a considerable number of the most respectable persons assembled admitted into the body of the sacred edifice. One of these was Miss Mitchell, the young lady whom we first introduced to the notice of our readers.

Remaining in the chancel after the others had passed through, she was invited by the beadle to take a seat near the altar. At first she declined, but, after a moment's hesitation, entered the church and took her seat in a pew from whence an excellent view of the imposing ceremony could be obtained.

The whole body of mendicants was now in commotion. Every one seemed anxious to obtain that position where he was most likely to attract the notice of the charitable. Instead of entering the church as usual, Mr. Scrieve and a number of mendicants took their places at the bottom of the steps, and were presently followed by his mysterious friend Muffle with the singular cane.

A few moments afterwards two carriages drew up at the entrance of the passage, and the wedding party entered the church. It consisted of the affianced couple, and a train by no means numerous or brilliant. They proceeded to the altar, took the places arranged for them, and the ceremony commenced. The silence which reigned in every part of the sacred edifice, rendered the clear slow voice of the minister quite audible throughout.

The performance of that holy rite seemed a matter of the utmost indifference to the two principals engaged in it. Each had their own motives for consenting to the contract, but the ceremony itself could scarcely be said to have created any of those pleasing emotions in either, which the mystical rite usually inspires.

Harriet Elizabeth, the daughter and heiress of Gregory Gripe, Esq., who at that moment had been united to the Right Honourable Viscount Victor Vernon, son and heir to the Marquis of Minchington, was not by any means beautiful. Tall and slender, with a pale sharp countenance, there was nothing fascinating or striking in her appearance; her dull grey eyes, surmounted by thin eyelashes, seemed heavy and spiritless. Nevertheless, her pouting lips and pointed features revealed considerable firmness and decision of character; at the same time the ensemble of her physiognomy portrayed extreme energy and haughtiness of disposition. She was attired in robes both magnificent and suited to the occasion, and moved with a proud mien, without seeming to attach any value to the superb display of her riches.

Viscount Vernon, to whom she had just given her hand, united in his person all the outward fascinations which nature is capable of lavishing. The regularity and distinction of his features; the rich proportions and real elegance of his figure, added to an affable and charming expression of countenance, contrasted strangely with those of his bride. In the midst of the young gentlemen who formed his cortege, one would have said that his evident superiority, and exquisite beauty, rather than a somewhat trivial circumstance, had chosen him to occupy the place of honour on the present occasion. A passing cloud of anxiety and fatigue was clearly perceptible on his handsome features; but it simply depicted the traces of recent suffering, and the expression which then reigned on the countenance of the viscount was replete with resignation and affability.

Detained at home by old age and infirmity, Mr. Gripe was unable to form one of the party; but he was most ably represented by the bridegroom's father, who saw with extreme satisfaction the restoration of his house to its former splendour, by the rich marriage of his son.

The Marquis of Minchington, whose ancient name had been partially obscured by intemperate extravagance and excess of every description, now carried his grey head, which was ravaged by anxiety, with that degree of pride and indifference for which he had been remarkable in his younger days. Seated in a conspicuous position, he looked on every side in order to show himself to the best advantage. In the absence of those admirable and fine moral feelings, which troubled him but seldom, he occupied himself by turning between his fingers a magnificent gold snuff-box, like a child playing with its toy.

The ceremony terminated, and all ranged themselves in order to leave the church, but the departure of the retinue was slowly effected. Now was the propitious moment for the band of mendicants, and each of them prepared to take advantage thereof.

The first hand which presented itself was that of the pretty Jenny. Lively, arch, and bold, the young girl unceremoniously threw herself before the newly-married couple, and earnestly solicited alms for "her suffering parent." In that doleful appeal, the rich tones of her charming voice contrasted strangely with the lamentable accent with which it was uttered.

That child of misery, notwithstanding her wretched figure, appeared so enchanting, that the Viscount could not refrain from regarding her with considerable interest. He sought for the largest coin in his possession, and accompanied the gift with a pleasing smile.

The mendicants pressed forward from every side, and their lamentable concert resounded throughout the passages surrounding the church. One alone among them remained silent,—it was Autumn, who, standing in the front rank, with an air of indifference, attracted thereby the notice of the Viscount. The latter regarded him with a searching look, and was about to make some observation, when Autumn moving forward a step, whispered the name of an individual in his ear, at the same time pointing to the corner where the infirm old Mary was seated.

Leaving his bride for a moment, the young nobleman hastened to the spot indicated, and there found the old woman crouched in an attitude of painful resignation. As he approached, the poor mendicant started with surprise; but when he threw into her apron a piece or two of gold, her face became illumined by an expression of irresolute joy, and a tear quickly coming to her eye, rolled down her cold pale face. Then in a moment of exuberant gratitude, which contrasted singularly with her previous melancholy depression, she seized the gift with a trembling hand, kissed it, and placed the treasure in the bosom of her gown.

The Viscount, gratified and affected, was about to address some kind words to the poor creature, when a piercing scream from the carriage attracted his attention and drew him away.

While that simple incident was passing in the corner, another of a more tragic character occurred at the other extremity of the passage.

Around the handsome equipage of the newly-married couple which had been drawn up close to the steps, a great portion of the assemblage were grouped. On one side, near the carriage wheels, Mr. Scrieve might be seen standing conspicuously forward, almost surrounded by a band of mendicants who enveloped, as it were, the dark figure we have described as Mr. Muffle.

Thoroughly occupied with the more interesting proceedings of the moment, no one noticed the transactions of "the gentleman in black." Without appearing to move, however, he slowly raised the mysterious cane, of which we have already spoken, parted it into two pieces, and stealthily projected one portion between the side and arm of his friend Scrieve, who stood immediately before him.

"Are you ready?" enquired the latter in a whisper, at the same time adjusting the point of the cane towards the carriage-door, in such a manner that it could not be seen by any one. "She is coming alone, by jingo!"

"All right," muttered Mr. Muffle, in reply.

A moment afterwards the bride approached her carriage, followed by the Marquis of Minchington and several attendants. As she was stepping into the coach, a slight whizzing sound might have been heard proceeding from the strange cane (which in fact was an air gun), and the next instant the Viscountess Vernon fell into the coach mortally wounded.

In the tumult which ensued, Muffle, protected by the mendicants, effected a safe retreat, muttering in a tone of extreme gratification as he escaped—"Revenged at last!"

The poor stricken bride lingered for a few hours, but before the rising sun illumined the darkness of the following morning, she had rendered up her life, and thus made the Viscount Vernon a bridegroom and widower in a day.

As the mendicants withdrew, they congratulated themselves on their success that morning, and joyously repeated to each other as they separated,—"To-night at the Three Topers."

—o—

CHAPTER II.

CAPTAIN CABLE AND HIS CREW AT THE THAMES TAP—THE BLIND MAN AND HIS PROTEGE—A TRIP THROUGH THE FOG—BATTLE OF THE BOATS—A NARROW ESCAPE.

IN one of those narrow and obscure thoroughfares which formerly surrounded the Tower of London, a remarkable dwelling stood conspicuous amidst its gloomy neighbours. Its projecting front, enlivened by fresh colouring, and the general air of comfort that pervaded the whole, contrasted strangely with the gloomy houses of the street, and gave it a cheerful and substantial appearance. Over the door hung a huge signboard, which bore upon its shining sides in glaring colours the following inscription : "THE THAMES TAP."

It was one of the most thriving public houses of that populous district, and, as might have been expected from its situation in Water Street, was usually filled with persons whose occupations were connected with the river or shipping.

It could scarcely be called a tavern, though, it is true, the worthy landlady dispensed both wine and liquors in considerable quantities.

As the old Dutch clock over the fire-place monotonously struck the hour of five in the afternoon subsequent to the events we have just related, the jovial Captain Cable arrived and established himself in the parlour of the Thames Tap.

The captain was a tall person—at least six feet high, and bore the appearance of an individual accustomed to the good things of this world. He was attired in the dark blue jacket and white trowsers usually worn by watermen.

Seated alone, on the other side of the parlour, was a man about forty or forty-five years of age, tall, with a calm and honest expression of countenance. He wore a decent costume, without any pretension to elegance, and altogether appeared to be a person in moderate but independent circumstances. He was a constant visitor to that house, where he was known as Blind Bolton, and generally regarded with mixed feelings of pity and esteem.

Mrs. Mouthy, the haughty landlady of the Tap, came from her citadel in the bar to greet the captain on his entrance, and exchange a friendly word with that best of customers.

A young girl, who appeared to occupy the position of barmaid, or upper servant of the establishment, stood leaning against the door in a thoughtful mood. She was exquisitely beautiful. Around her handsome forehead shone a halo of calm and serene dignity; her long jet-black hair fell in rich curls over her beautifully-modelled shoulders, and the outline of her magnificent figure preserved a latent but exquisite gracefulness, which added materially to the proud perfections of her features. Her fine black eyes remained fixed and motionless, like those of a somnambulist, betraying evidence of profound reflection.

It was on this exquisite form that the sightless eyes of Blind Bolton appeared incessantly fixed. As he sat sipping his sweetened wine his lips would move, and he seemed to discuss those internal thoughts which are common to persons deprived of sight.

In the tap-room, and near the bar, a number of persons, whose disordered costumes resembled those of Thames watermen, were drinking together. Those about the bar formed the crew of the jocular Captain Cable.

"Mary (cried the captain), Mary, my dear, mix me a stout can of brandy and water. I like plenty of sugar, ye know."

But the beautiful girl did not appear to hear the order that was thus addressed to her, for she neither spoke nor moved.

"I say, Mary," roared Captain Cable; then, as the lovely barmaid still remained immovable, he continued, in a tone of vexation, "I'll be d——d if she will hear me to-night. Once more, will you brew me another can of grog? I shall be obliged to call up Mother Mouthy, if you don't set about it soon; and it strikes me ye wouldn't like that, my lady!"

After waiting a few moments to see if his orders were obeyed, the captain approached the steps leading to the cellar, whither the landlady had retreated, and called—

"Mrs. Mouthy! Mrs. Mouthy!"

The great lady of the Thames Tap entered with step at once majestic and solemn. She was very short and stout, and the exercise of ascending the stairs had lent to her features a rosy healthiness.

"The d——l take me! (said Cable, as the landlady approached,) but the Thunderer might fire a forty-eight pounder in the ear of your young lady there, without making her stir."

"Mary!" cried Mrs. Mouthy, in a loud voice.

A slightly perceptible trembling agitated the eyelashes of the blind man, and a faint shadow overspread his countenance. The young girl, however, did not move.

"Look ye, Mrs. Mouthy, (resumed the captain), I'll lay ten to one she wouldn't deign to reply to the Lord Mayor of London himself!"

As the captain thus gave vent to his chagrin, Mrs. Mouthy approached the meditative Mary, and shook her roughly by the arm.

"What d'ye mean by this sulking?" she exclaimed, in an angry tone.

The young girl recoiled a step, and became purple with indignation at the brutal attack of her mistress. Still silent, she replied to the angry hostess with such a gesture of pride and true dignity, that the latter was incapable of uttering a word.

At that moment the blind man smiled and rubbed his hands, as though something extremely gratifying had occurred.

The pretty Mary, however, immediately resumed her mournful and indifferent attitude. The brilliancy of her splendid black eyes became somewhat obscured, and Mrs. Mouthy felt her courage return.

"Give bread to an unfortunate hussy (said she), or take into your house a naked mendicant, and, by way of thanks for such charitable relief, she will ruin your place, and drive away your customers."

"Leave the poor girl, Mrs. Mouthy, and give me my grog."

The hostess obeyed, but, offended at the unusual tone of authority in which the captain had spoken, determined to have her revenge.

The blind man swallowed at one draught the remainder of his wine. "I would not have missed this for a thousand pounds," murmured he.

As the neighbouring church clock struck six the individuals who were drinking at the bar began to move away, and one of them, a short herculean-looking fellow, advanced to the parlour door with an inquiring glance. The captain arose.

"Well, Dick my boy (said the latter, buttoning up his jacket); come along, old chap. Ah, there is the pretty slut, Mary, who will not hear us, you see, Mrs. Mouthy. I hope she will be in a better humour when we come back. I shall return this evening as usual, my dear hostess. Be so good as to prepare my grog against I come; you know how."

The captain took his cane and followed the watermen into Lower Thames Street, the only wide thoroughfare which separated them from the river. The sailors proceeded in small groups of three and four each, singing loudly as they went along in a feigned style of intoxication. The captain followed about twenty yards behind them. On passing the Custom-house, they perceived two or three officers, who were smoking to while away the hours of duty. Cable touched his hat as he approached them. "Happy fellows, Mr. Moore," he observed, pointing to the sailors.

"Ay, ay, sir (replied the officer); jolly rascals, every one."

"A deuced fog to-night," observed Cable.

"The devil's own mist, sir."

The captain proceeded on leisurely while within sight of the officers, but the moment they could no longer perceive him, quickened his pace, and rejoined the sailors in a deserted alley, which led to the Thames at the end of Bobbin Lane. They passed down the alley in profound silence, and reached the dilapidated and unfrequented stairs at the bottom without being observed. On arriving at that forsaken spot, the captain cast around him a careful and searching glance, but nothing suspicious was perceptible. He then made a sign to the sailors, who noiselessly began to descend the steps.

"Who mounts guard, to-night?" demanded Cable.

Two men immediately stepped forward.

"Pusey and Groper, eh? Good! Watch well, my lads (resumed the captain). Now for the boats."

The two men to whom the captain thus addressed himself, remained on the top of the steps, unfolded the large cloaks which they carried on their arms, and enveloping themselves therein, lay down on the ground like two inanimate logs of wood. Captain Cable and the other sailors divided themselves into three parties, and each took possession of a boat with a black sharp keel, whose gunwale was scarcely perceptible above the level of the water.

"Muffle the oars," whispered Cable, who commanded the principal boat. "Now, row boys, row."

The three boats silently quitted the water side, tacked about, and with difficulty found a passage

through the small craft of every description which encumbered the banks of the Thames. Sometimes they glided under the gigantic prow of a merchant-man; anon they passed a dark and deserted collier; and occasionally their oars got entangled in the fastenings of the numerous boats and cables which they met with on every side.

A dense fog, impregnated with the heavy vapours arising from innumerable fires on the river, enveloped them on all sides. Nearly all the lights of the vessels at anchor were extinguished. There was no one visible either on the lighters or other small craft afloat.

Beyond the vessels thus abandoned for the night, or only guarded by a somnolent watchman, the dimmed lights exhibited at intervals the scarlet casement of a tavern, from whence proceeded sounds of harmony or lugubrious intoxication.

The three boats gradually and silently ascended the river.

"The devil take me, if it isn't fine weather for business, Billy my boy," said the captain, in passing under an arch of London bridge.

"Fine, capt'in, werry fine, (replied the robust Billy Bull); but the tide's nearly reached its height."

"And the breeze will rise with the ebb," added one of the rowers, whose exuberant corpulency almost filled the whole width of the boat; "we must lose no time, for the fog will not continue long."

"Let's make haste, fat Dick," said a very precocious little fellow, who answered to the lively appellation of Weasel. "Besides, ve vant to settle 'counts vith the guvnor. Our fobs is empty, and it's unpossible to get on vithout ribbon, as Black Bob says."

"Silence, you son of a brigand (exclaimed the captain), silence my dear boy—the less we speak of the governor the better—but I wonder what has become of that damned scoundrel, the dearly beloved fellow, Black Bob ?"

"He's got marrid (replied Dick), marrid in St. Giles' to a thing six fut high without her shoes ! We shaun't see much of him now."

"Ah ! (exclaimed little Weasel,) master Bob is more cunning than ve be; he verks on his own account, and goes to the autumns on Sunday evenins—there's many good things to be done in autumns, ye know."

"Peace little devil, silence my boy," interrupted the captain in his usual style of amusing contradiction. "We are under Blackfriars Bridge, where there's plenty of watchmen walking about."

The boats quickly issued from the thick gloom which reigned under the arch, and the two sides of the river were again perceptible.

"Ho, ho, (exclaimed Billy Bull,) three lights ! yes, there they be—it's all right; and ve shaunt have too much for the three boats, I see."

The lights of which Billy spoke were clearly distinguishable through the gloomy fog; one of them was perceptible under Blackfriars Bridge, the second glittered on the opposite side of the river, about a quarter of a mile higher up, and the third hung from a post near the steps of the Red House in Southwark. All three shone with great brilliancy, and though surrounded by lights and fires of every description, were easily discovered by those who knew them, without being detected by others.

"We must separate (observed the captain); I shall call upon that old rascal, Cabbage, and see what he has in his confounded public-house, the Blue Dragon, long life to him ! You must proceed to the Black Cat, Stringer; and you to the Red Hand, Boxer; and mind you keep your ogles open."

In obedience to these instructions one of the boats moved towards the Surrey side of the river, and the second proceeded in an opposite direction; that of the captain continued to ascend the river.

"No blue light to-night :" remarked Dick.

"That's lucky (replied the captain); I don't like to see the blue lantern myself—I always fancy I hear the last cries of some poor devil being strangled when that is shown. It's a weakness, no doubt, but when I see that blue-eyed monster, I always change my mixed grog for the neat article itself, in order to raise my spirits. You laugh at

it, Billy, do you ? Well, it always costs me a shilling more in grog on those occasions, and that's an object."

"Vel, (said Dick, with indifference,) vot does it matter about a backer (death) more or less ?"

"Nothin at all," replied little Weasel, laughing.

"Every one must live, captain (added Bull); if our three queer buffers (publicans in league with thieves and murderers) did not do a little in the slaughtering bisiness, vot would the doctors do ?"

"For my part I'm fond of the blue-lantern," said Weasel.

"Well, I must say (murmured Cable), for one so young, that sweet youth is the most venomous reptile I ever knew. Look out, Billy, look out there."

The boat, which for some time had floated alone, was now steered into that labyrinth of lighters, barges, and pleasure-boats, which encumbered the sides of the river. Billy handled the oar very cleverly—Dick seized the helm, and the boat touched the shore without any impediment. The place where it stopped formed a sort of small harbour, protected by the projection of a lofty house, partly constructed on piles over the water, and partly on terra firma. It was that house which bore the lantern with green rays.

Captain Cable searched between the enormous piles which supported the dwelling, and found a ring attached to the end of an iron chain; upon giving this a vigorous pull, the feeble sound of a bell was heard over his head. At the termination of a few moments a creaking noise was heard just over the boat.

"Who's there ?" inquired a voice prudently disguised.

"A comrade, my dear Cabbage (replied the captain), the devil take me, but I'm glad to see you to-night. How goes it at the Blue Dragon ?"

The captain was interrupted in his friendly inquiries by a rough blow given him by a bale, which was descending at the end of a long rope.

"What the devil are you about, Cabbage ?" he murmured ill-humouredly, "mayest thou slip thyself through that infernal trap-door of thine, some fine foggy evening like this."

While thus grumbling he quickly slipped aside, and his men detaching the bale, threw it into the bottom of the boat, and the rope was again raised by Cabbage.

"That smells all musk (said Dick); it's the stuffin' of a oak's peter, (the contents of a gentleman's portmanteau,) I'm sure. I say, Billy, make fast the spring pump afore the keel's filled."

"The sucker plays famously, don't it ? I should not like to have a bathing this cold weather," replied the fat rower.

"Good night!" exclaimed the voice from above, in a morose tone.

The trap-door was again lowered and secured.

"Row away, boys (commanded the captain). It seems to me that the fog is rising—good night, old vampire—thou nocturnal butcher and miserable strangler, good night (continued he on leaving the shore). But here is our boat from the Black Cat—Ho! ho! there."

"Ho! ho! it is. Six bales, captin."

"Good! Now row away, boys,—stop, I perceive that confounded scamp, Boxer, our worthy comrade. Ho! ho! there."

"Ho! ho! (replied the person hailed). Only two little parcels, captain."

"Two small parcels!" repeated Cable, with a disconcerted air.

The three boats then proceeded on their course down the river. The tide being in their favour, they rapidly approached the arches of London Bridge. A slight breeze had risen with the ebb, and the fog appeared to be clearing up.

"Our game is likely to be rather awkward (remarked Dick); ve shall be twigged by the light of the lamps, I'm afeard, and if ve be, the peepers (Custom-house officers) will be out."

"Row away, Dick, my lad, you fat porpoise, row (said the captain), a few more strokes of the oar, and we shall be hidden behind the hull of that large three-masted vessel, unless"——

The captain suddenly interrupted himself, drew a deep sigh, and then continued—"The water must be very cold for a bath, my lads, nevertheless, it strikes me we shall have a dip to-night."

The boat then left the middle of the river and glided under the shadow of the merchantman. The men ceased rowing, and were within two hundred yards of the place from whence they had started, when the captain, after listening a moment, turned to the little oarsman, saying, "Call, Weasel."

In a moment a shrill and wonderfully modulated mewing emanated from the feet of the anxious captain. A few seconds afterwards a dull whining bark was heard proceeding from the river side.

"D——n! (muttered Cable between his set teeth;) we are stopped! But after all it may be a mistake. That devil of a fellow Groper barks so well, that one never knows whether the sounds come from him or some poor dog wandering through the street. Try again, Weasel."

The cry of a cat was imitated a second time with ncreased force and perspicuity. Again the barking was heard in reply.

"It's Groper, that's clear (observed Bull, in an under tone). Them d——d peepers is afloat somewhere atween us and the steps."

"The devil take those Custom-house men (added Cable angrily); come, my lads, we must prepare to meet them; luckily the breeze has slackened, and the fog is returning as thick as ever. Now steady awhile."

The other two boats drew up alongside Cable's, and all three remained stationary under cover of a large vessel, while preparations were being made for active defence. Captain Cable took a small round package from the locker of his boat, and unfolding it upon his knee, exhibited a mask, so admirably constructed that it was impossible to detect its disguise. Having arranged this to his satisfaction, he next exchanged his blue jacket for one of a coarser texture, and after effecting sundry other metamorphoses, took up a short cutlas, saying, "Are you ready, my lads?"

"Ay, ay, captain," said Stringer and Boxer at the same time.

"Well, then (resumed the captain), you had better give us those two parcels and advance against the enemy with your empty boat, Boxer, my boy; perhaps we may thereby escape. You follow us, Stringer. Now, forward."

The three vessels struck off at once, but at the same time that the leading boat issued from the shade, a black mass doubled the prow of the merchantman.

"Ho! there, (cried a commanding voice;) who's that out at this time?"

"Only two or three vatermen returnin' from a short cruise," replied Boxer, hoping to gain time for his comrades to escape.

"Heave to, and let us see you (commanded the voice), that is, if it be possible in this confounded thick fog."

Boxer slowly obeyed, and an officer was about to enter his boat with the view to search it, but just as he stepped on the gunwale, a sudden jerk from something under the prow shook the craft, and threw him into the river.

"Halloo! (exclaimed the officer in command of the second Custom-house boat,) there's a rat in the trap somewhere! I'll leave you, Harry, to pick up master Crab, and settle with those black looking dogs, while I go in search of the sneaking reptile that is kicking in the chain."

After Boxer had separated from his commander, the latter slowly advanced on the opposite side of the river.

"Tack about, Billy," said Captain Cable, in an under tone.

The little craft replied to the combined efforts of the watermen, and darted towards the river side with unusual velocity. But a heavy, chain purposely drawn across that part of the river, struck with great violence the bows of the boat, and instantly arrested its progress. That shock affected others as we have seen.

"Cut it in two, Bill (said Cable), or by—"

The captain checked himself, and proceeded to steady the boat, whilst his men dealt heavy blows upon the object which obstructed their further progress.

"It's a great chain," murmured Dick, savagely.

"Ho! ho!" cried a voice approaching.

No one replied; Cable drew his cap over his brow, and adjusted the cutlas that hung in his girdle.

"We must get her over or under it (whispered he to his men). But the devil take me if I wish to have a bath this evening. It's no use talking, however, so here goes! Come along my lads."

Without further hesitation Cable plunged into the water, followed by his crew. By a vigorous and united effort, they had nearly succeeded in their object, when the chain suddenly gave way and left them comparatively free. At the same moment, however, the black mass previously observed, which, as we have seen, proved to be a Custom-house watch-boat, was rapidly advancing to meet them, and an engagement seemed perfectly inevitable. Hastily re-entering their vessel, Cable and his crew once more prepared for battle.

"Who goes there?" demanded the officer, in a commanding tone.

No one answered.

"What boat is that?" repeated the voice.

Still no answer.

"Stop!"

Captain Cable appeared to take no notice of that command. He, however, cast an inquiring glance towards the vessel from whence it proceeded.

"There are eight to our five, my lads," he said, in an under tone.

"But veen got two fives! (said Weasel, in a similar voice); and I'm sure Stringer isn't afeard of a little skirmishing."

"True, my dear little viper (rejoined Cable); we shall lick them between us, at that rate."

The Captain now turned to the other boat, and exclaimed. "Look out, my worthy blood hounds! here they come."

"Ay, ay, captain (replied Stringer); all right here."

The approaching craft seemed much larger than that of Cable, and, as the captain had remarked, was manned by eight stout men, well armed. The commanding officer directed its course against the further progress of the advancing boats, and the crews met each other with a bold and determined front.

"What have you there?" demanded the officer, as his vessel ran alongside that of Cable.

"You had better come and see, my fine fellow, if it is particular;" replied the Captain, in a tone of defiance.

Without further ceremony the officer prepared to accept the challenge thus offered him, and was about to step on the gunwale of Cable's boat, when his crew were suddenly attacked in the rear by Stringer and his companions.

The contest immediately became general. Captain Cable, taking advantage of his numerical superiority, fought with a skill and courage truly astonishing. He knew perfectly well that it was a matter of life or death with himself and all connected with the illegal transactions in which they were engaged. He consequently contended with a degree of bravery with which desperation alone could have invested him.

The engagement was short and decisive. Whilst defending themselves on one side, the government crew were violently attacked on the other, and one or two were soon precipitated into the river, from whence they with difficulty arose. Wounded in several places, as were most of his crew, the custom house officer found himself utterly incapable of preventing the escape of his opponents, who hastened to avail themselves of the opportunity afforded them.

While this conflict was taking place, the crew of the other watch-boat were busily endeavouring to rescue their commander from a watery grave; but the tide running rapidly at the time, it became a matter of some difficulty, and a considerable time elapsed before they succeeded; during this period Boxer and his companions, profiting by the confusion, reached the deserted stairs, where Captain Cable and his two crews arrived almost at the same time.

"The devil take me if we havn't had enough for one night," said the captain, placing his foot upon the steps.

The captain was slightly wounded in the arm and breast. Weasel shook like a drowning spaniel; he, too, was wounded, but complained more of the wet than the cuts he had received. Ascending the steps he gave a feeble mew, and hearing the bark of Groper in reply, hastened to the latter and thrust himself into his cloak. The others placed the packages on their shoulders, and passed through the gloomy alleys in the neighbourhood of the Tower, but took care to avoid the custom house on this occasion.

Cable hastened home to change his wet clothes and dress his wounds, and then proceeded to the Thames Tap, as if nothing unusual had occurred.

At the moment he entered the parlour, a violent noise was heard proceeding from the lips of Mrs. Mouthy. That lady had never been very remarkable for a patient temper, and being driven to desperation by the quiet indifference of her handsome bar-maid, raised her hand, which fell with brutal force on the pale cheek of poor Mary.

"The devil take her (muttered Cable), that will prevent me getting my grog."

The blind man had not stirred during our nautical and exciting excursion. He had been supplied with a second and a third glass of his favourite beverage; and doubtless heard the effect of the blow, for he abruptly rose, and his face, commonly inanimate, suddenly assumed an expression of strange and excited wrath.

"She is a virago!" he muttered.

Mary appeared to experience a terrible shock; her livid features became somewhat contracted, and a gloomy light shone in the depth of her eye. Her robust nature instinctively revolted against the outrage she had experienced. One might have supposed she was about to bound forward and strike her assailant.

"Ah! ah! (exclaimed the captain,) I'll wager two to one, that my worthy friend will receive her deserts."

Mrs. Mouthy thought so too, for the deep carmine of her cheek gave place to a visible palor, and she could not avoid trembling. But the beautiful girl seeing her triumph, crossed her arms on her chest and smiled with contempt. A sigh of relief escaped the blind man.

Without saying a word to any one Mary passed the bar and slowly ascended the stairs leading to her bed room. Bolton threw half-a-crown on the counter, forgot to ask for his change, and departed, groping his way out.

"Come (said the jovial captain), my amiable friend has escaped her nicely! As to poor Mary, she will have a place of lodging for the night, thanks to that devil, Blind Bolton, provided he does not break his neck first."

Whilst standing outside the door, Bolton heard a light foot passing in the direction of Thames street, and immediately followed it. Mary's step though light was firm, and struck the ground at regular intervals. By the pale light of the lamps the beauty of her form was exhibited in fantastic perfection. Bolton followed her cautiously, as though some mysterious instinct illumined his eyes.

On emerging from Lower Thames street, Mary took the same dark road that the sailors had taken, and entered into the narrow lane which led to the river. Bolton hastened forward and caught her, as she arrived within a short distance of the water.

"Where are you going, my child?" he inquired, in a tone of friendly solicitude.

"To the river!" replied Mary, without once pausing.

These were the first words that Bolton had heard her utter during the day. Her voice, always sweet and melodious, now appeared to participate in the solemn expression of her face.

"To the river! (repeated Bolton). Do you then think of drowning yourself?"

"Yes!" returned Mary, with a profound sigh.

"Why, my daughter; wherefore do you wish to die?"

"Because I have neither hope for the future, nor an asylum for the present."

"I will give you an asylum, Mary, and offer you hope."

"Others have frequently spoken to me thus," she replied, casting upon her companion a melancholy smile. "They wished to purchase me, but I am not for sale. That is doubtless your object."

"God forbid, my child."

The poor girl was about to traverse the few steps that still separated her from the river, but Bolton seized her arm, saying with evident emotion, "Are you not afraid to destroy yourself?"

"No!" she replied.

"What has your mother taught you?"

"Nothing! I am the child of singularly strange and unfortunate parents."

"You are ignorant, I imagine, of all concerning them?" observed Bolton.

"No (replied Mary); my father was immensely rich before—before—he died (she continued in a tremulous voice); and I was taught to dress, dance, sing, and speak several languages."

"Were you happy then?"

"Oh, yes! I led a contented life."

"And if I were to restore you to that life?"

"You!" exclaimed the young girl, in a tone of lively solicitude; then resuming a melancholy air continued, "but alas! there are so many that have already spoken to me thus, that I have no hope left. No, my heart and body belongs to one that is dearer to me than life."

"But I neither demand thy heart nor body, child (observed Bolton). I am blind and cannot see thy perfections."

"Neither my heart nor body? (she resumed,) and you are blind! Then what do you desire of me?"

"I desire thy good-will only."

The young girl reclined her beautiful head on her bosom, and stood for a moment in profound reflection; then turning to her companion, she continued in a tone of deep pathos: "One day I fell, dying with fatigue and hunger, at the steps of the

Thames Tap, and the house of that woman who just now gave vent to her brutal passions, received me. In exchange for my liberty she gave me bread; in return for my services I obtained bread; for incessant abuse I received bread! It was bread, bread, nothing but bread!"

"If you accept my offer (said Bolton), the treatment will be widely different."

"What do you require me to do?"

Bolton drew from his pocket a well-filled purse, and presented it to Mary.

"Listen to me attentively (said he). I engage you not for myself, who am weak, but for a society which is both strong and terrible. I have been acquainted with you from your infancy, and know you better, perhaps, than you know yourself. You must be silent with regard to our meeting. As to your duties, they will be extremely easy—all that will be required of you is fidelity and passive obedience. Retire this evening whither you please. This day week knock at the door indicated by the address on this card. It will immediately be opened, when you will enter its mistress, for that house will be yours! Good night, Mary, you will see me again!"

—o—

CHAPTER III.

THE THREE TOPERS—A RENDEZVOUS OF THE MENDICANTS.

A SHORT distance from the top of Field-lane,—a dirty narrow passage, leading out of Holborn, and in a crowd of obscure thoroughfares, of which Saffron Hill formed the central point; one, if possible, more wretched than the rest, was remarkable for the number of low public-houses it contained. Near the middle of this street stood a dull, heavy-looking tavern, designated "The Three Topers." Its worm-eaten, creviced front, showed that it might once have been painted of a deep red-colour, but time and dirt had so ravaged its exterior features, that this circumstance became a matter of doubt. Its low, narrow windows, with small panes, and muddy frames, rendered it extremely dark and uninviting.

But it was almost always full, and the landlord became a prosperous man. After having passed the threshold of this house, one approached the bar, which was generally surrounded during the day by a lot of heterogeneous beings—scavengers, sweeps, itinerant merchants, Jews, labourers, and mendicants of every description. At the entrance by the bar was a narrow passage, leading to other apartments, but more especially to a large one denominated "The Club Room," wherein the mendicants of the district usually assembled to spend the night in revelry and dissipation.

It was striking ten, and a large fire burning in the wide grate of the club room illuminated every corner of that spacious apartment. A great number of the mendicants were assembled. Among those present were most of the persons whom we previously saw at the church of St. Simon. The morose Black Bob was there, dividing his attentions between a jug of ale and a black-eyed female, not overburthened with dress; the philosophic Timbers shone to advantage amidst his less volatile companions. The negro Cæsar, who, thanks to some unknown source, was enabled to pay his score and treat his comrades, never failed attending the rendezvous of the mendicants. Seated near the fire, Mr. Muffle appeared to contemplate the blazing coals with profound attention, interrupted occasionally by the lively sallies of an interesting girl near him. The warlike boatmen Bull, Weasel, Groper, and their comrades were also there, engaged in fighting over again the battle of the boats. Lastly, the cold and calculating Autumn, seated at a separate table, was conversing with the pretty Jenny and her mother.

A great change had taken place in the general appearance of these mendicants, some of whom were so metamorphosed, that their own companions could scarcely recognise them. One no longer saw those patched eyes, wooden legs, or arm stumps that were met with at every corner of the street; on the contrary, the blind could now see—the lame walk, and even dance; those whom we had seen exhibit but one hand for the gratuities of the generous, now showed two powerful "mawleys," that would have done honour to a coalheaver. The poor weak voice, which solicited alms in doleful accents during the day, was here exerted with boisterous effect in songs and revelry. The halt no longer limped; the maimed appeared whole; "the lepers were cleansed, and the deaf heard"—all were singularly transformed from extreme wretchedness to apparent felicity.

How these extraordinary changes in the personal characteristics of the mendicants had been effected is one of the leading purposes of this tale to describe. But we must not anticipate.

While the mendicants were busily engaged in discussing alike the qualities of the refreshments, and their schemes for the following day's operations on the sympathies of the generous, a personage of some importance in their fraternity entered, and with an air of condescension took his seat amongst them.

"Ah! ah! (exclaimed the jovial Timbers) how is our worthy friend Mr. Scrieve—he's come to honour us with his company to night! Good morning to you, sir," continued the merry fellow, who, by his humorous contradictions, merry disposition, and being almost the only real cripple present, had become the chartered libertine of his party.

"Good day, good day," replied Scrieve coldly.

"Nasty morning—stars shine beautiful to-night;" added Timbers, with a glance at Jenny.

"Fine night enough," added Scrieve, as he paid for a foaming can of grog which was just then placed before him; "how's business?"

"You needn't ask that (interrupted Mrs. Malpas); only look at Timbers and you'll be quite satisfied there."

"Ha! ha! (resumed the latter) Mother Malpas was always more fond of a joke than a jug! For my part, I like both."

"Devil doubt it!" interrupted Autumn.

"Well! between the devil and the Church, I manage to scrape along somehow," added the jolly Timbers.

"But you always seem very happy and comfortable," said Scrieve, in a deprecating tone.

"So I am (replied Timbers); I don't scrieve doleful strips (write piteous letters), saying I was once happy, &c., &c."

"Well, well, old boy, don't be offended."

"Devil a bit of it (said Timbers, laughing); here's yer health, me hearty, and success to the last lines ye sent."

And the facetious mendicant tossed off a bumper as he uttered the words.

"Here, Polly," cried Cæsar, as the dirty waitress was leaving the room; "three cans more grog—hot, sweet, an' strong; I'll pay for it!"

"Bravo, Tawney! (exclaimed a sinister-looking mendicant near the negro,) go it my tulip; business is brisk with yer, aint it?"

"Can't say so, (replied the negro, with a sigh.) Them damned pals of mine wont let me get anything if they can help it—if there's any balsam (money) to be given, they prevent me from havin' a share."

"It ain't made for you, Tawney."

"No, my fine gentry cove, so it seems; you beats me now, but rec'lect we'll be equal agin when we gets to the old house (grave); there black and white turns tawney both on 'em. Howsomever, I gets on, ye see, in spite of all."

"But you black devils spile our business."

"That ain't true, 'cause ye vont let a body try it on. Howsomever, when I comes and spends my tin, ye treats me as one of yer best pals."

"Ha! ha! (vociferated Timbers) its the king's pictures we respect, and not your'n."

"I knows it, I knows it," replied Cæsar, with a deep sigh.

"Never mind, old boy, (added Timbers, in a consoling tone), I didn't mean to hurt your feelings. Take a swig at the grog to raise yer spirits, and I'll tip ye a stave to help it, eh?"

"Ay, ay, a song!" cried the mendicants.

Timbers took a long draught at the liquor by way of preparation, and then chanted the following lines.

"When darkman[1] draws the curtain round
The scenes that in our life abound,
                      Both fair and foul;
And all have left the busy streets,
Here every pal his doxy[2] meets,
                      With a full bowl.

When we have cast away our rags,
The lifters[3], stumps[4], and mealy bags,
                      Patches and paint;
Maunders[5] and prigs[6] in jolly throng,
With foaming grog and merry song,
                      Come benculs[7] quaint.

Here we will throw our cares away,
Let cacklers[8] rant and parsons pray,
                      Juggle and prance.
Let the bowl pass round before us,
With hearty voice join all in chorus,
                      Laugh, sing, and dance.

"Bravo! bravo!" exclaimed the mendicants.

"More humpty, dumpty," (ale boiled with brandy,) cried Jenny.

The favourite beverage was soon supplied, and the can went round amid the din and laughter of the assembled mendicants. After a brief interval, the waitress was again called by Autumn.

"Polly, (said he,) let's have three cans of stammer (brandy and wine, mulled and sweetened), and don't be afraid of stirring your stumps, or I'll tip ye a little maundering broth (abuse), when ye come with it."

"Ah! (exclaimed Scrieve,) so I see it's true what's said about your long ribbon (much money), my boy."

"Let 'em say what they likes, (replied Autumn,) but in reality none on 'em knows anything at all about me or mine."

"That's the reason why folks talk of ye," remarked Mrs. Malpas.

"And a werry good 'un too," added a mendicant.

"Ay, ay, (said Timbers,) and it's a sort of punishment for keeping secrets. Come, come, let's have a 'full, true, and particular account of yer life, trials, and—and—well, yer executions,' old boy."

"Faith, that would be soon done," said Autumn, emptying his can, and reflecting for a moment. "So ye want to know my history, do ye?"

---

[1] Night.   [2] Mistress.   [3] Crutches.
[4] Wooden legs.   [5] Mendicants.   [6] Thieves.
[7] Friends.   [8] Dissenters.

"Ay, ay," replied several voices.

"Well, then, set the percher (listen) and look out for squalls. I was born in a sort of cooland (desert), near the soldiers' barracks (sea side). While a kinchen (child), I loaped (ran) about over the waste, and as soon as I was big enough, they made me lag the blacks (watch the crows). I never saw any one but my parents, and them only at times. When still quite a kid (young), I was sent out to work in the nearest coops (fields), from lightman to darkman (morning till night), and as I was one day digging near the root of a very old tree, found a libbege of spanks (bed of gold)."

"Spanks?" interrupted several mendicants, anxiously.

"Ay, real king's pictures!"

"A big heart (large treasure)?"

"P'raps it wouldn't have been a heart at all to anybody but me," replied Autumn, with a thoughtful air.

"A heart, a big heart?" repeated the mendicants anxiously.

"Yes, (resumed Autumn,) I found quite enough under that tree to set us all up, and give me a new life. Our cabin was soon changed into a beautiful cottage; the country all round it was cooped and planted; and everything looked neat and comfortable. My father and me lived there many years as happy as a bug in a rug, and the place seemed to get prettier every day. We couldn't have wished for better luck—it was good, too good to last," continued Autumn with a sigh.

"Take a swig, old boy, (suggested Timbers,) it'll cheer ye up and carry ye through."

This advice was adopted, and Autumn then proceeded with his narrative.

"Well, (said he,) time jogged along, and we was hoping to live and die in peace, on the spot we had found so comfortable; but one stormy day, the salt lay (sea) burst over the shore, reached our crib, and with a single stroke of its cursed wave destroyed all we had or hoped for."

"Balsam and all?" inquired a voice.

"Everything (replied Autumn, as he drained his can). My father was drowned, and I had hard work to save myself. Without ken or grub (house or food), I was forced to tramp off after it.

"Well, (he resumed, after a brief pause,) I moaped about for two or three days, living only on balls (turnips), and such things as I could pick up; but this couldn't last long, so I made for the nearest ken I could find. Just as I reached the gigger (door) there was a tramper (gipsey), who had been a mumping (begging) herself; and, hearing me ask for some panum and rowd (bread and cheese), she stopped to snith (see) if I would get it. But the old topcussin (farmer) wouldn't tip us a mite, and so we come away together.

"'You aint a reg'ler maunder?' said the tramper.

"No (says I), it's the first time as I ever asked for anything, and its hard to be refused, when a body's almost dying with want.

"'Dying for want! (said the tramper,) and such lots of barnacles (good things), all about ye?'

"'Barnacles!' says I.

"'Yes,' repeated the dimbermort (pretty girl); and if you'll come along with me I'll prove it.'

"So away we went together till we comes to the mouth (entrance) of a thick wood, which we entered, and after groping through the roughmans (brambles) for some time, arrived at a part that looked like a smuggen (cavern). It had been partly cleared in front, and seemed a snug little place, where stiffing and autumn (murder and marriage) could be managed comfortably.

"'Be ye game to venture in that 'ere crib?' said the dimbermort, smiling at me.

"'Oh! ay,' says I; for I thought if it was a trap to bone Jack Adams (catch a fool), it couldn't be worse than famishing.

"Well, in we goes, now stooping, now creeping, and now walking upright, through the darkmans. We went round, forard, and sideways; and as we was proceeding, I heard a sort of groan, as if a stiffing was going on, and fell down frightened to death.

"'What's the matter with ye?' asked the tramper, laughing hearty.

"'Didn't you hear a noise?' said I, trembling dreadfully.

"'What sort of noise?' says she.

"'A deep moan, like somebody dying.'

"The minute I uttered that word my companion left me, and did'nt return for more than half an hour. I tried to grope my way back in the dark, but it was no use, for I had got into a gin of doubles (maze of passages), and was regularly fixed. I was just beginnin' to think it was all up with me, when I twigged a light coming towards the place where the tramper must have left me.

"'Where's he got to?' cried the dimbermort, searching about.

"I stood still for a minute, not knowing whether to answer or not; but my tommy-tub (stomach) began to rattle so loud, that I was forced to call out.

"'Here,' cried the tramper: 'but in the Ruffin's (devil's) name shake off them awful looks, or I'll leave ye to die, instead of taking you to a jolly stuff (meal).'"

"But what about the noise?" enquired Timbers.

"Wait a bit," replied Autumn; who, being supplied with a fresh can of his favourite beverage, took a long draught, and then resumed.

"Well! reminded by my pipes (bowels) that I mustn't lose the chance of a good tuck-out, I made a sort of laugh of it, saying I was cold and hungry, but should be all right by and bye.

" 'Come along, then (said the dimbermort, talking in a whisper). This is the blue (northern) ken of our Maunderoi (King of the mendicants); but he isn't here now, though one of the culls (chiefs) is, and if ye likes to join us he'll span (enrol) ye.'

"So I followed her till we comes to what seemed like a ruff (bush), when my tramper lays hold on a particular branch, and give it a twist. The ruff in a moment fell on one side, and a gigger opened, showing us five or six maunders, with their comfortable impudences and kenchens (wives and children), sitting round a glorious spread.

" 'Here's the jackram,' (poor novice,) 'says my

linker (guide), taking me up to a stout fellow with a red nab (cap).

"After speering (scrutinising) me from nab to stamps, the cull (for he was the leader) give a grunt of satisfaction, and told me to set to. The dimbermort then took me to her set, and give me a large bowl of smoking hot olios (a hash of game, poultry, pork, mutton and vegetables, stewed together) which was a thousand times pleasanter because I had long wanted grub.

"Well, I worked away at the olios, and was picking the last bone of a fine fat gobbler (turkey), when I hears another groan from the doubles. Down goes my bone and bowl in the fright, and the red nab seeing it, gives two blows on the floor, and two of the mummers took me into another room. I was ready to drop with fright at this, but my linkers forced me to drink something hot and strong, which had a very wonderful effect on my spirits.

3

" ' You're better, now ?' said one of the maunders.

" ' Ay; but what was that groaning ? ' says I, innocently.

" The mummers looked at one another for a minute or so, and then one of 'em replied, ' Oh, that's the bleating of a cow's baby.'

" It may be so, thinks I, but it certainly don't sound much like it. However, it's no good contradicting these mummers.

" ' You don't seem like the kid of a oak,' (a rich man's child,) said one of 'em, twigging my looks.

" ' No (says I), neither have I got any cub or trumps,' (home or friends).

" ' Well, my boy (said one of 'em, kindly), we'll be yer trumps, if ye like. What say you ?'

" ' I shall be very glad if ye will,' says I.

" ' But ye must join our camp,' said the other maunder.

" ' Oh, I'm willing enough,' I replied, recollecting how well they had treated me.

" Then they took me into a fine room, with a good fire burning, and everything looking cheerful and comfortable. There was a large day sleeper (easy chair) near the table, and matting down each side of the room. On the shelves was lots of books, and cases, and several pictures hung on the walls, with a portrait of the Maunderoi over the fire-place.

" ' Have ye quite made up yer mind to join us ? (inquired one of the mummers). Recollect, there'll be no flinching afterward.'

" Yes, I know all about it,' says I, for I had heard of their rules and laws long before.

" The two maunders then left me alone for more than half an hour; but, thinking I was in the king's room, I didn't dare to stir from the spot where I stood, for fear I should be nabbed for so doing.

" By and bye they returned with the whole tribe at the time staying there. I was regularly entered and admitted into their band in the name of Autumn. I took the oaths to obey the Maunderoi and his laws; to keep the secrets of the fraternity, and to defend it against its enemies as far as I was able.

" Ay, aye; in coorse," cried the mendicants.

" Well, the chief then made a speech on my admission.

" ' You shall be received and protected (said he) wherever ye may meet with any of our band, and will join us in all our glories, as long as ye remain faithful and true. Should ye cab (desert), however, or use the velvet (tongue) squarish (foolishly) against us, it'll be worse for ye; but if ye turn jude (traitor), and betray a pal, yer punishment will be ——

"Just at that moment, the groaning which had frightened me so much afore, was again repeated, but in a weaker strain. The chief then pointed in the direction from whence the sounds proceeded, and said—

" ' Yes, if ye turn jude, I repeat, yer punishment will be like that of the wretch who is now dying for his duds (treason). Go, then, and success attend ye. Yer two new pals, Cherts (ears) and Burr (dependant) will set ye out.

" I stopped about three months along with the band without any thing worth mentioning takin' place. At the end of that period, I went out one darkmaus with my pals Burr and Cherts to boune a baler (sheep) for the gag (pot). We went to the coops of that damber (rascal) topcussin who had refused me grub, and boned (stole) his mort (best).

"I was in coorse suspected of bein' one of the prigs, and finding that the bandogs (officers) was out arter us, we three stamps off for London, where I've been ever since, and where, as it seems, I am likely to stop."

" Your history is strange and curious," remarked the pretty Jenny.

" And not too clear," added Mrs. Malpas.

For the last few moments Mr. Scrieve had not been listening to the conversation, but regarded Jenny with his cold dull eye, without uttering a single word.

" Mrs. Malpas," said he at length.

" Well ?"

" It strikes me your daughter could do much better than go mumping about through the streets in that ugly toggery (dress) of hers."

" I don't know that," observed Mrs. Malpas.

" I'm sure I get lots of ribbon," said the smiling Jenny.

" How much did ye get last week ?" inquired Scrieve.

" Let's see," said Jenny, reflecting a moment; then calculating the amount on her fingers, resumed—

" On Monday, one trooper (half-a-crown), one bord (shilling), two crokers (fourpence), and a grig (farthing); Tuesday, one George (half-a-crown), two dace (two pence), and a bawbee (half-penny); Wednesday, a coach-wheel (half-a-crown), two bob (shillings), and a thrum (three pence); Thursday, three bord, three treswins (three pence), and three grig; Friday, a George, one bob, one tanner (sixpence), and a bawbee; Saturday, a bull (crown), one rub (a penny), and a bawbee; Sunday, half a meg (half a guinea), a flag (fourpence), and two grig. Tottle—one king (sovereign), one George, one duck (ninepence), one tanner, and one bawbee."

" One pound, four, and ninepence halfpenny, in vulgar reckoning (remarked Scrieve, musingly). It's good—very fair indeed, as things go. But she must do better than that."

" How?" inquired Jenny and her mother at once.

" Come hither, (said Scrieve without noticing the anxious glances cast towards him by the mother). Yes, (he continued), she'll do admirably !"

And he took the smiling Jenny, turned her about in every way as if he were playing with a top, and resumed—

" She must be sent to certain bobkens (great houses) with a good ticket (character), representing her to be the only daughter of dancing (paralytic) parents, or the oldest sister of twelve fatherless children."

Then, without waiting for the reply of Mrs. Malpus, who was laughing with an amused air, he began to place the young girl in a variety of attitudes; teaching her to assume with facility, the most affecting and miserable positions. He instructed her in the art of fainting; of calling tears to her eyes, and the banishment of colour from her rosy cheeks. By his advice, she learned to modulate her voice to every purpose, and to assume a manner in accordance with the object of the moment.

Jenny, who at first received these instructions with considerable indifference, opened her fine eyes widely when she was informed that henceforth she should wear better dresses, and go to visit great persons.

" Ah ! (she exclaimed, striking the table with delight,) I will positively go to the bobken of that nutty gentry cove who got autum—"

" Stop, Jenny (interrupted Scrieve); you mustn't talk of bobkens and gentry coves at such places."

" But I'll go there first, won't I ? He looked at me so droll when leaving the aut— well ! the church I mean."

" You think so, do ye ?" said Mrs. Malpus.

" I'm sure of it (replied Jenny, with a laugh); for he felt in his bung (purse) for a piece of spanks, gold I mean (continued Jenny, correcting herself on perceiving her tutor frown). I don't know why, but somehow I feel sure he'll tip—that is, give me more."

" Ah ! (exclaimed one of the mendicants near them), if it's Lord Vernon ye are a talking of, that is a ken worth trying, I knows."

" That don't concern you," observed Scrieve.

" It is Jenny's house," added Autumn.

" But there's room enough for others too (growled the mendicant); besides, I've been there afore."

" Are you in a position, then, to present yerself in a drawing room ?" inquired Scrieve, in a sarcastic tone.

" Never mind, master Inky (replied the mendicant in a surly tone); I gets vot I vonts."

" So does I, ven I goos there," added another of the band, not more prepossessing than his companion.

" No nonsense, boys, (cried the merry cripple); it ain't worth while quarrellin' about, seeing as how there's room for all of us as likes to try it on."

During that colloquy, other mendicants assembled together in little coteries, were occupied in a somewhat similar manner. Some were singing, and others laughing at the jokes of their companions; but the far greater portion appeared to be engaged in discussing their schemes of operation for the following and succeeding days.

One group in particular, consisting of the famous Black Bob and his worthy friends Weasel and Bull, who had retired to an obscure corner of the room, seemed profoundly occupied in the preparation of some grand project.

" Well, my lads (observed the former, after a pause), I'm quite villin' to jine ye in the bisniss, perwidin' ye helps me in mine."

" In coorse (replied Bull); that's fair."

" But vot does the doctor give for a subject ?" inquired Black Bob.

" Five megs (guineas) for a stiff 'un (the body of a murdered person), and two for a poor backer," (one that died), replied Weasel.

" Good : and now that's settled, let's talk over the other job," said Bob.

" Goo a head, me tulip."

" A gentry cove vonts two dimbermorts looped off."

" Two at once !" exclaimed Bull, with surprise.

" Vy, not exactly (replied Black Bob); leastways, not for hisself. But they be both livin' together, and I vos thinkin' that vile servin' the genl'man vith one, ve might werry vell do a little bisniss on our own account vith the other !"

" I twig," said Bull and Weasel together.

" Vell, my lads, what says you ?"

" Agreed !" replied Bull.

" Yes, ye may depend on us two (added Weasel); but vhen's the job to be done ?"

" Oh ! werry soon. But I must see the guvner fust."

" So must we soon (observed Weasel), seeing as how the ribbon's gettin' short."

The mendicants continued their orgies throughout the night; but when the cold, raw air of morning penetrated the pestiferous fumes which arose from the drunken revellers that remained, nearly all the leading characters of our story had departed to their own dwellings.

CHAPTER IV.

LOVE AND JEALOUSY—A MYSTERIOUS CHARACTER.

One Sunday evening subsequent to the victorious escape of Captain Cable and his confederates from the Custom-house boats, Mr. Dawson, a Welshman by birth and a physician by profession, escorted his two fair cousins to their parish church.

These young ladies, being very religious and charitable, were extremely regular in their attendance at divine worship. Caroline and Jane Jones were amiable, accomplished, and very beautiful. Their father, a popular country gentleman, resided at Holywell House, and held the commission of the peace for the county of Glamorgan. Their education had partaken of a strongly religious character, and their whole time appeared to be occupied in pious and charitable pursuits. They resided with Dr. Dawson's mother, their aunt, who was as pious and moral as themselves.

The good lady's house was visited only by a few sedate, charitable ladies, by no means gay or pleasant. They were frequently joined by the Rev. Richard Roby, the minister of their parish, who became much attached to the two sisters.

On the Sunday evening of which we write, Mrs. Dawson became slightly indisposed, and the doctor was consequently called upon to escort his fair cousins to church. Warmly attached to both, but more especially so to the fair Caroline, for whom he felt a regard approaching that of love, the young physician gaily descended the steps of their residence, not a little proud at having on each arm one of his charming cousins.

Dr. Dawson was a fine young man of twenty-five, with agreeable, regular features, and handsome figure. He had been in practice about five years, and was gradually becoming celebrated in his profession. His cheerful and gentlemanly manners gained for him the good opinion of all who knew him.

Although he was thus esteemed a worthy person and good Christian, yet the doctor had the strongest antipathy to what he secretly termed the prosy monotony of his friend, the Rev. Richard Roby's sermons, and consequently but seldom attended to hear them.

As they approached the church the physician began to lose a little of that gaiety for which he was remarkable, and soon fell into a thoughtful mood. As faithful historians, we feel bound to record the fact that his present gloom arose more from an unconquerable dislike to encounter the formidable sermon than any other cause. A few moments' reflection, however, enabled him to arrange a plan for escaping it.

"Dear me!" he exclaimed, with well-feigned surprise, "how provoking! Really, cousins, I am a great blunderer."

"How so?" demanded Jane.

"Because I have forgotten to visit one of my patients."

"Do so to-morrow," said Caroline.

"To-morrow? it may in all probability be too late."

"You will rejoin us soon?" observed Jane, in a tone of inquiry, as she entered the porch.

"Assuredly."

"Caroline seemed somewhat cold and indifferent (murmured Dr. Dawson, as his cousins entered the church). I perceive she could easily dispense with my protection."

We trust that the reader will not hastily form an unfavourable opinion of Dr. Dawson, who is destined to occupy an important position in this narrative, if we at once admit that he had no patient whatever to visit that evening,—the Rev. Richard Roby's sermon had alarmed him, that was all. It was very wrong on his part, undoubtedly, but then there are excuses for young doctors only twenty-five years of age. Instead of listening to the worthy minister, he projected a snug little chat over a pipe in the chimney-corner of a neighbouring friend, or probably a walk on the bridge, or perchance something else; but Caroline's apparent indifference had given him food for reflection, and prevented that determination. After strolling about for a short time, he returned to the church, and noiselessly glided behind the pillars of the choir. He stationed himself in a position where, without being seen, he could observe the motions of his cousins.

The church they attended was one of those fine old Gothic structures erected in the age of Catholic ascendancy, having the usual dark passages and secluded avenues to be found only in edifices of that description. St. Mary's had been filled at the morning's service, but in the evening there were few present except the Rev. Richard Roby's own flock, almost entirely composed of elderly ladies, who, however, nearly filled the interior of the choir.

For some minutes Dr. Dawson did not perceive any thing calculated to attract his attention. The two young girls, kneeling in their pew, were absorbed in prayer. The Rev. Richard Roby slowly and solemnly proceeded with the service, his congregation repeating, at proper intervals, their grave responses. When the minister had concluded, the congregation rose, and then only did Dr. Dawson discover the faces of his cousins. Before sitting down to listen to the sermon, Jane cast one or two benevolent smiles towards her acquaintances; Caroline, on the contrary, did not think proper to imitate her example, but turned towards the pillar against which her cousin was leaning. At the moment her eyes appeared to reach that object, she started; her head bent down, and a sudden paleness chased the fresh colour from her cheeks.

"I am an awkward fellow! (muttered Dawson to himself); she is startled at seeing me here."

By an intuitive movement he again concealed himself behind the pillar; but, after the lapse of a few moments, he once more cautiously thrust forth his head.

Caroline remained in the same position; and although the minister had commenced his sermon, she had not resumed her seat. A mysterious influence seemed to render her perfectly immoveable, and her piercing look appeared rivetted to the pillar.

"That is strange (thought Dawson); I have never before observed her look thus."

After he had twice repeated that remark, he asked himself the question which another, probably, would have ventured before.

"Is it me whom she is regarding?"

To ascertain this, he walked rapidly round the pillar, and in doing so, suddenly found himself in the presence of a mysterious-looking personage, who was supporting his head against the column. That man's eyes were closed, and a vague smile played on his lips.

Dawson started with surprise, and became pale in his turn. He cast a rapid glance towards Caroline, but her back was now turned towards him; she had, in fact, reseated herself.

But Jane replied to his anxious glance with a look which doubtless meant—"Very good, cousin, your patient has not detained you long, it seems."

The most profound anguish then began to penetrate the heart of Dr. Dawson. He had hitherto loved Caroline from association only, but now she appeared to be the sole object of his life, and essentially necessary to his future happiness. There was no more doubt or hesitation. On Jane he did not bestow even a single thought. His forehead became heated, and his heart beat with a violence hitherto unknown.

He remained in a state of doubtful consciousness for several moments, almost annihilated by the severe blow which had just stricken him, and made a vigorous effort to shake off the feeling of jealousy which appeared to be creeping upon him, but without success. After contemplating for a moment the drowsy figure which he believed to be his rival, he mentally declared a war to the death.

The unconscious sleeper, however, did not of course suspect it. His eyes remained closed, and his mouth preserved its pleasing smile. The doctor was almost tempted to touch his arm, and call him out for satisfaction; but what motive could he give for the challenge? Besides, the physician, as a prudent man, began to inquire whether such a proceeding would answer the object in view. Now, Dr. Dawson was undoubtedly a brave young man, but his professional avocations had rendered him extremely cool and logical; he could not avoid, therefore, asking himself this question :—

"Suppose I call him out, and we fight? If I kill him there is an end of the matter, and my enemy is destroyed! But the probabilities are, that he will kill me! Am I avenged? Malediction! No; that would be adding crime to injury."

The mysterious individual who was leaning against the pillar, and had thus become the object of Dr. Dawson's regards, appeared to be a model of supple and muscular vigour. He was evidently a young man of about twenty-five or thirty years of age, with a tall and elegant figure, and of a decidedly aristocratic exterior. His attire, designed with a view to the utmost simplicity, but with marvellous taste, resembled the dress of those who are slaves to fashion. His countenance presented a remarkable type of beauty and intelligence. His large high forehead, of peculiar vivacity, but traversed from top to bottom by a slight scar, almost imperceptible except when much excited, was crowned by a head of magnificent black hair. His eyes were not perceptible, but their fine dark lashes presaged extreme power. His handsome mouth, now partly open by the smile that played on his lips, was surmounted by a fine black moustache, which reminded one very much of the Spanish bandit, and exhibited to view a brilliant range of small white teeth, that would have done honour to a lady. These features, somewhat too delicate, perhaps, and surmounted by two sharp eyebrows, as dark as his hair, lent him an aspect of firmness and hauteur. In short, he was one of those men whose magnetic profiles glide into romances for the express purpose of setting at naught virtues the most impregnable—a second Don Juan; and yet it is doubtful whether that renowned personage had been so lavishly endowed by nature.

Leaning against the column in a careless attitude, he seemed to be sleeping, if not dreaming of something very agreeable, for his physiognomy appeared to reflect a series of fugitive and pleasing sensations.

Dawson contemplated this mysterious personage for some moments with extreme vexation. The young physician was himself a very good-looking person, but like all lovers who are absorbed in their own prospects, the idea did not once strike him that a parallel might be established between himself and that magnificent stranger. His jealousy represented himself more perfect than he really was, and detracted from the merits of his supposed rival. In this view he thought that those closed eyes might be blood-shot, and, carried away by that false hope, he silently chuckled to himself—" He probably squints !"

That idea, vague as it was, sensibly calmed his excited feelings, and as the sermon, of which he had not heard one word, was drawing to a conclusion, he abruptly left the handsome dreamer to observe more closely the deportment of his cousins.

Scarcely was he at his old post when the whole congregation arose from their seats. The young physician, now burning with jealous excitement, cautiously watched every movement of the sisters, and his whole soul seemed to pass into his eyes, which shone with an extraordinary brilliancy.

On rising, Caroline once more cast an inquiring glance towards the unfortunate pillar. Again was her look steadfast, piercing, and full of interest. Dawson would have given six years of his life to be regarded thus; and, anxious to know how the sleeper would respond to it, retraced his steps for that purpose. But the stranger continued his somnolent position, apparently regardless of what was taking place.

" It is strange (thought the doctor)—he does not even see her, who appears to think but little of me by the side of that obscure individual." The poor young man felt profoundly humiliated in that reflection.

" He is ignorant of his conquest (murmured Dawson stamping with rage); it is she who is in love, and not that mysterious creature ! Alas ! he has vanquished me without knowing it !"

That supposition keenly wounded the sensitive heart of the young physician, and a cold perspiration flowed from his furrowed brow. He envied the heroes of the melodramatic theatres, who strut about the stage with poison in their pockets, or a dirk by their side, for the purpose of represssenting the perpetration of suicide when necessary.

As the congregation commenced the doxology, Caroline turned towards the altar with evident regret—she would have contemplated a little longer the pleasing features of the unknown.

At the first note of the sacred harmony which issued from the choir, our sleepy stranger opened his eyes, and smiled with a gratified air. His countenance expressed a sort of vague ecstacy which exhibited still more vividly his handsome features.

At the conclusion of the sacred music, a soft step was heard behind the physician, and a sweet voice whispered—" For the benefit of our charity schools."

He turned round and beheld Jane with a plate, which she immediately held towards him for a subscription. Dawson, seized by an excess of prodigality, threw noisily on the plate one after the other, two pieces of gold.

Jane thanked him with a gracious smile. After that act of romantic generosity, the doctor somewhat recovered his spirits, and breathed more freely. He then cast a triumphant glance towards his mysterious rival.

" In that I shall at least surpass this hateful unknown !" he murmured.

" For our charities," again said Jane, as she stopped before the stranger. The latter started at the sight of the beautiful mendicant, and raised his hand to his brow as a person who believes himself to be the plaything of an illusion; then stedfastly regarding the young girl, he remained for a moment immovable.

Jane, bashful, and blushing, was about to retire, but the stranger retained her by a gesture replete with graceful politeness, and, taking from his pocket a richly embroidered purse, selected therefrom a ten-pound note, which he placed on the plate, at the same time bowing with profound respect.

At the sight of this, the physician seemed petrified with astonishment; he clenched his fingers convulsively, and bit his lips till they bled.

" Ten pounds !! (he murmured,) and I only two."

There was another who had noticed that munificent gift, and regarded with a longing eye the gorgeous purse from whence it had been taken ; but he was at that moment scarcely visible amidst the darkness of the cloistered passages which filled the sacred edifice.

The stranger followed Jane with an ardent look whilst she continued to solicit subscriptions. When she became lost in the crowd, he took a hasty glance at those around him, and, amongst others, his eyes fell with indifference on the features of Dr. Dawson.

" He does not squint ! (thought the latter ;) but where have I seen that figure ?"

It was in vain that he endeavoured to recollect, and he finally concluded that some vague resemblance had led him into an error.

The shades of evening had completely set in, and that part of the church where the congregation was assembled, was brilliantly lighted up, whilst the nave and aisles were lost in darkness.

The handsome stranger having been interrupted

in the enjoyment of his reverie, left the spot where he had stood, and slowly proceeded towards one of the aisles.

At the same moment, a man, very badly attired, and with a suspicious mien, stealthily glided past. Instead of following our illustrious dreamer, however, that man took an opposite direction, and proceeded in such a manner that in all probability they would meet each other in the most secluded and obscure part of the church.

Dr. Dawson had observed all. At first he thought that a murder,—in the event of his suspicions being well-founded, would marvellously serve his interest; but he was a man of education and honour, and repressed the selfish sentiment the moment it invaded his mind. In his turn he left the pillar, and entered the shades of the aisles, resolved, if necessary, to lend a loyal succour to his unknown rival.

Dr. Dawson followed the stranger for some time, but the aisles were plunged into so profound an obscurity, that at a distance of ten yards it was impossible to distinguish anything before him; and he, consequently, soon lost sight of his unknown rival, whom he was unable to trace any further. He then proceeded towards the other aisle, for the purpose of arresting the wretch whom he anticipated was about to commit an awful sacrilege; but without succeding in his object.

The handsome stranger, however, ignorant alike of the danger which menaced him, and the generous solicitude of which he was the object, pursued his enchanted promenade. He quickly arrived at a secluded part of the aisle, which being covered with a coarse matting, destroyed the sound of his footsteps, and prevented the physician from tracing his course. At that spot the notes of the sacred music reached him as they died away in solemn harmony; and he abandoned himself to the pleasing emotion of the moment. He reposed for awhile from an agitated, and, probably, a very guilty life; for our stranger was an extraordinary individual, as we shall have frequent occasion to exemplify.

Mysterious and reserved, when it suited his purpose, he was also solemn and indifferent in moments of partial repose. A man of pleasure and voluptuousness, he could make himself a Christian for one hour, to taste the emotions of a vague and delicious mysticism. He would sometimes become benevolent in order to enjoy the happiness of doing good; at others, he would amuse himself with the exercise of a power which but few in this world have ever possessed. He was a man of strange sensations, who knew how to extract enjoyment from everything—a man at once capable of good and evil; generous by character—

open and enthusiastic by nature—cold by calculation, and of a disposition to sell the world, with his own soul, for a quarter of an hour's pleasure.

Although his life, hitherto, had been a strange compound of good and evil—of gratified passions and realised caprices, his heart and mind had preserved an exquisite sensibility. He took love in small drafts, as a connoiseur takes wine; his hatred, when perchance he became malignant, was dear to him; and his vengeance, though not perhaps of that brutal nature which ordinary persons employ, was yet terrible in the extreme. Those who did not know him in either of his multifarious characters, admired, loved, or respected him; those who perchance knew, or fancied they knew him, could not resist his extraordinary power, but bent before his iron will.

On the day in question, he had a whim for solemn reverie, and determined to enjoy it. The next he would probably smile with disgust at the thought of it.

As he seated himself on a bench in that obscure aisle, our stranger fancied he heard a slight noise behind him, but took no further notice of it, for at that moment other ideas of a more pleasing character invaded his brain, in the midst of which the same sounds, but approaching still nearer, again struck his ear; it seemed like the creeping of something heavy over the matting. The unknown remained immoveable, but his ethereal dreams at once evaporated, and that vigorous mind, which immediately returned to its state of reality, coldly examined his situation. By a slow, continued, and imperceptible movement, he turned his head, and perceived a dark figure creeping towards him.

" That rascal has robbed me of my reflections (thought he); he wants to assassinate me, no doubt. Humph !"

In mentally giving expression to these words, a brief smile of contempt overspread his lips, but he did not move. After the lapse of a few seconds, the individual who was thus crawling towards him, and who was the ill dressed personage to whom we have before alluded, suddenly rose and sprang upon the stranger; but his dirk, although well directed, only struck the back of the bench, for the unknown, quickly leaping on one side, avoided the mortal blow. At the moment that the assassin was about to recover himself, he felt his wrist pressed as if by a vice.

" Oh! (cried he, in doleful accents,) I thought there wasn't sich another fist as mine in the whole world; but, oh! I'm damnably mistaken though."

He carelessly approached his face close to that of the stranger, and, their eyes, being habituated to obscurity, immediately recognised each other.

"What, Black Bob!" muttered our handsome unknown.

"Mercy! my lord, mercy! (cried the assassin, trembling with fear, as he instantly fell upon his knees,) I didn't know you, my lord, indeed I didn't."

His lordship then dropped the arm of Black Bob with a smile of contempt, and the latter immediately joined his hands in a supplicating manner.

"My lord! my good master! (cried he;) with that dress you look as slender as a young lady, and it's unpossible I could know ye in it."

"Is that a reason why you should commit murder? and in a church, too!"

"I am starvin, my lord: you do not often pay us, my good master, (continued Bob, in a tremulous and supplicating tone;) times is very bad in London, and it's hard to get a livin' anyhow. *In the Welsh mountains, now —*"

"Silence! (interrupted the unknown, in a commanding voice, which made the assassin tremble from head to foot;) what are thy comrades doing now?"

"Not much, my lord; times is very bad."

"Go to the house to-morrow, and you shall be paid; but, by Satan! no more of these tricks, master Bob!"

His lordship proceeded towards the side of the choir, where the congregation were singing the last verse of the Dismission. He was closely followed by Black Bob, whose hands were thrust into his pockets, and his head bent downwards, like a dog which had just received the correction of its master.

Dr. Dawson had regained the opposite side of the church almost at the same moment, and it was with indescribable surprise that he beheld the handsome stranger return to the choir, accompanied by the black-looking wretch he had previously noticed. Now that the danger of assassination was past, all his ideas of vexation and hatred resumed their ascendancy, and he almost repented of his former uneasiness on the subject.

The stranger approached the altar with a solemn and aristocratic air. He paused before the congregation, and, dropping one of his superb gloves as he was about to draw it over his sinewey fingers, undertook the long and difficult operation of thrusting them into another.

Black Bob picked up the fallen glove, and humbly presented it to the unknown.

While replacing it over his fingers, the latter cast a glance of mingled interest and admiration towards the blushing Jane, whose eloquent appeals to the charitable had rendered the fair mendicant so successful that evening. But he did not appear to perceive Caroline, whose look had not left him for a moment. Dr. Dawson, on the other hand, did not notice Jane, for jealousy made his blood boil, and obscured the usual brilliancy of his vision.

Before leaving, the stranger placed a glass to his eye, murmuring as he did so,

"She is decidedly beautiful — nay, absolutely ravishing!" He then motioned his follower to approach him. "Do you perceive that pretty girl near the pulpit?" whispered the unknown, when Bob was near enough to hear him.

"I sees a great many."

"But the most beautiful of those two in dark-looking dresses?"

"That's accordin' to fancy, my lord."

"She who is now closing her prayer book, I mean. Do you observe?"

"What, the lady who was just now begging for the charities?"

"Exactly."

"What a capital mendicant she must be to get ten-pun' notes!" observed Bob, in a tone of admiration.

"Silence! (murmured the stranger,) you will follow her, and to-morrow bring me all the information you know I require respecting her."

"Yes, my lord."

The unknown having finished putting on his gloves, proceeded towards the door, and passed Dr. Dawson without noticing the hateful looks which the latter cast towards him. Caroline still followed him with her eyes as long as he was visible.

Scarcely had he left, when the physician, hastening from his retreat, abruptly presented himself before Black Bob.

"The name of that man who has just left you?" he demanded.

"He is not a man!" replied Bob, coldly.

"What then?" inquired the physician, with surprise.

"A mystery!"

"Nonsense! (exclaimed Dawson, in a tone of vexation); who is he, I ask?"

"I don't know."

The physician plunged his hand into his pocket, and withdrew therefrom two half-sovereigns, which he secretly slipped in the hands of Black Bob.

"Oh! that alters the case (observed the latter, as he placed the money in his pocket). You want to know his name, do ye?"

"Yes; be quick!"

"He's got two thousand seven hundred and odd, I believe; which will ye have?"

"Pooh! pooh! I want his real name."

"I don't know it."

"Not know it?" observed the doctor, in an incredulous and mortified tone.

"It aint' likely as he'd let me into all his se-

crets (suggested Bob). Howsomever, I thank ye kindly for yer charity. May God bless ye, young gentleman," he added, bowing, and then disappeared like a shot.

—o—

CHAPTER V.

THE LION OF THE DAY.

Our scene now changes to a more aristocratic part of the mighty metropolis. From the busy abodes of industry and strife, of affluence and wretchedness, which compose the great capital of England, we now turn our steps towards its western extremity.

Littlemore House was one of those doubtful-looking mansions whose dark brick exterior, surrounded by high walls, but feebly indicated the station of its proprietor.

Lord Littlemore, to whom it belonged, however,

was a nobleman by birth and fortune. His ancestors had held important positions in the state, and he himself had represented his country at one of the principal courts of Europe. Upon returning from his diplomatic mission, he retired into private life, and his drawing-rooms were the rendezvous of the political party to which he belonged. He was a widower, and confided the direction of his household to Lady Longton, who also undertook the education of the Hon. Miss Littlemore, his only daughter.

Lady Longton had once been extremely beautiful, though in 17—, the epoch wherein our history passes, she had lost a considerable portion of her charms, but neither the ability nor desire to please. She was no coquet, and quite as little of a prude —a woman of wit and fine taste, she had good-humouredly cast aside every outward pretension to youth, and scrupulously attired herself in a style suitable to her position.

4

The Hon. Miss Littlemore, her niece, was about eighteen years of age; rather tall, and of a slender figure. She was very handsome, but her beauty partook of that sweet and feeble nature which we find so frequently pourtrayed on the canvas of Sir Joshua Reynolds, and which we sometimes espy behind the windows of an emblazoned equipage. Her complexion was of a transparent and pearl-like whiteness, now and then brightened up by a slight roseate shade; but it seldom attained that lively colouring which is symptomatic of vigour and health. The translucence of her features was remarkable around her eyes, where it assumed a pale blue coloured reflection. Her blond hair, of extreme elegance, fell in slight curls over her fair cheeks. Her fine eyes of tender blue, were sometimes partly closed, and then seemed to be swimming in a humid and scintillating medium. Her smile was that of a child, but when she became serious, a tremulous curl on either side of her lips gave to her mouth an expression of disdain.

The Hon. Miss Littlemore was thus endowed by nature; but education had given her new and far more attractive charms.

Under the careful tuition of her aunt, she became an accomplished and amiable personage. Naturally timid and diffident, modesty gave her an air of reserve foreign to her disposition. Such as she had become, however, was entirely owing to the judicious instruction of Lady Longton, who was justly proud of her work, and jealous beyond measure of the despotic power she exercised over her niece.

The Hon. Miss Littlemore was an only child, and a great heiress. Her father possessed an income of seventy thousand a year—some people affirmed that it was considerably more. Be that as it may, it was assuredly not less.

One may well suppose, therefore, that the heiress of such a fortune, even if not loved for her own sake, had, under the circumstances, a great number of admirers. Indeed, about two years previous, on her first entrance into society, she was surrounded by innumerable lovers. The most favoured of her courtiers had been a young man of very moderate fortune, but of princely origin. He was the youngest son of the Marquis of Minchington, and bore the family name of Vernon. He was the younger brother of Viscount Victor, whose marriage we have already described. The Hon. Miss Littlemore, or rather, Lady Longton, condescended to notice him, and, accordingly, people believed that the matter was arranged; but suddenly, a new and formidable competitor arose, and recommenced the struggle with astonishing vigour.

The powerful champion who had thus entered the lists, was no less a personage than the celebrated Duke de Duro, a grandee of Spain, France, and other states.

In the year 17—, the Duke de Duro, the most illustrious and distinguished personage of his age, returned to London. Every one knew the dazzling and incomparable Duke; everybody recollected the oriental magnificence he displayed during his residence in this country, as also that he expended twenty thousand pounds each winter; still, however, he was not a nabob.

The Duke was in the habit of visiting London every year; but one season passed without his appearance. Was he dead or ruined? No one could tell.

Most people imagined that he would some day reappear at his magnificent palace in London, with all his usual splendour. They lamented his absence, but could not prevent it.

One day in December 17—, the Duke de Duro arrived from Paris, where he had been staying during four or five successive winters, the king of fashion and the lion of the day. He came suddenly, as had been anticipated, and was followed by an army of lacqueys and retainers.

It is no ordinary circumstance that would set London in commotion. Foreign princes, and the sons of emperors have passed through its crowded streets unnoticed and unknown; Greeks, Turks or Indians scarcely attract more than a momentary attention, and it is even questionable whether a visit from the Emperor of China himself would create more than a nine days' wonder. To produce a great effect in the overgrown capital of old England, one must possess the powers of a magician or the wealth of Peru. De Duro, however, had neither the one nor the other—he appeared a simple duke.

The day after his arrival in London, he became the object of universal conversation. The western palaces prepared for his reception with anticipated delight; the city shopkeepers sung his praises in strains as varied as they were numerous; and the amazons of Billingsgate were equally voluble with his name. He was the subject of conversation in St. James's and St. Giles's—in Whitehall and in Smithfield.

Still, however, no one could boast of having seen this celebrated personage. The two or three first days after his arrival, were passed in retirement at the magnificent house which he usually occupied. Nevertheless, there were numerous reports concerning him at the reunions of fashionable houses in the neighbourhood of his mansion. Young noblemen related astounding anecdotes of the illustrious Duro. Among the assemblages of wealthy citizens, there were a few honest, demi-lions in their way, who knelt at the repetition of a name so distinguished. Finally, in the dark lanes of the country, in the low taverns of the metro-polis; in filthy huts and dirty streets—there were gloomy, ignoble wretches, who, in the intervals of dissipation or trouble, blubbered the same name, and with a degree of interest equally profound.

Thus in the universal excitement which pre-vailed, a deafening concert arose from the saloon, the anti-chamber, the shop, and the attic; and sent forth towards the cloudy sky of London the same name, a thousand times repeated, of De Duro!

Every one represented to himself the mysterious Duke according to the natural inclination of his own ideas. Elderly people, deceived by his name and reputation, expected to see him enveloped in the red cloak of Fra Diavolo, or, at least, the coarse plumed hat of Don Juan. Young ladies saw him in their dreams, with a thoughtful eye, a ravaged forehead, Roman nose, and divine smile. Lastly, old servants figured to themselves that he had curious rings on each finger, a grotesque cane, and watch seals worth five thousand pounds.

One may very well suppose, therefore, how much this mystery and excitement increased the desire of everybody [to know the Duke. It did not rest with any particular class or party, but was universal. The rich panted to behold that dis-tinguished personage who had held the sceptre of fashion both in Paris and Madrid; the aristocracy of the city longed for the reappearance of the greatest merchant of the age; and the Men-dicants, who knew him best, perhaps, prayed in silence for his coming.

It was supposed by some that his sudden arrival in this country had reference to a diplomatic mission of the highest importance; and it was consequently a matter of contention whether the Whigs or the Tories should receive his first visit. Innumerable were the invitations presented to him from all parts. He did not hasten to choose, how-ever; but one evening after paying a secret visit to a certain house in the city, he ordered his carriage, and drove very quietly to Mallington House.

Lady Elizabeth Lawson, Marchioness of Mal-lington, was the widow of a nobleman who had held a distinguished position in the history of his country. Her wealth almost rivalled that of the greatest bankers in Lombard-street. She appeared almost twenty-eight, and was acknowledged to be one of the most charming women of the day.

When the Duke de Duro was announced, a perceptible but mute emotion ran through the assemblage of ladies who lined the drawing-room of the Marchioness of Mallington. The younger portion seemed to tremble with a delicious curio-sity, and the others advanced their dowager-looking features between the blooming visages of their more juvenile associates. De Duro entered, and a slight disappointment was depicted on the coun-tenances of many. They undoubtedly deemed him handsome, but scarcely romantic enough. They seemed to have expected a more poetical mien, and a look less easy to define. But the moment he spoke, the charm operated with astonishing effect and a sort of reaction took place. The young ladies lost their hearts irrevocably in the electric current of his magic words, and the dowagers re-gretted the happy time when they might have enjoyed the same sensations.

Though some might have been somewhat dis-appointed at his personal appearance, all were dazzled by the royal splendour he displayed—not as an enriched merchant, or conceited fop, but a real nobleman of the most illustrious class. He, consequently, soon became in London what he had been in Paris and Madrid—the lion, the king, the god!

About the period of his arrival in England, several new debutantes had been introduced into the fashionable world—persons who bore distinguished names, and led remarkable lives. Amongst those whom we will cite, Captain Considine, Dr. Dawne, Sir Samuel Saunders, and Le Chevalier Curato. These gentlemen were well acquainted with the Duke, but neither appeared to be admitted into his immediate society.

It was reported that the first conquest De Duro had made, was in a quarter least expected. The Marchioness of Mallington had hitherto borne a most enviable reputation for a young widow. She was a woman of marvellous taste, a coquet the most dangerous in short, and the least likely to be attacked with success. In a world so busy with its slanders and calumnies, it is rather sur-prising that Lady Elizabeth should have lived so long without reproach. No stain, however trifling, had ever tarnished the virgin mirror of her renown; the men loved and feared her, and her rivals dreaded the effect of the superior attractions which she possessed. But when De Duro came, the very existence of the Marchioness was sud-denly enveloped in an unusual mystery, which envious tongues did not fail to render suspicious. She might have defended herself by a frank avowal of the real sentiments of her heart. But she loved De Duro with that sincere intensity which ever seeks to hide itself lest it fail to ensure a return of the feeling.

The Duke, however, loved her with equal

sincerity. But his passion was far too ardent to endure. "He came, he saw, and he conquered;" but was himself subdued at the same moment. With that impetuous sincerity and frankness for which he was peculiarly remarkable, De Duro threw himself at the feet of Lady Elizabeth, and vowed eternal love. But the Duke had deceived himself. Without reflecting for an instant on the consequences of such a proceeding, he had abandoned himself without reserve to the delicious excitement of the moment. But when time and reflection had somewhat reduced the intensity of his passion, he forsook the object with as little remorse as a child who neglects the plaything with which it has become satiated.

May providence preserve all those blooming creatures who so foolishly flutter about the fascinating halo of the Duke de Duro!

—o—

CHAPTER VI.

HOW THE DUKE DE DURO FELL IN LOVE, AND THEN FELL OUT AGAIN; BUT, NOT EXACTLY COMPREHENDING THE MATTER, PLUNGED ONCE MORE INTO IT.

THE circumstance of a marriage in high life creates a considerable sensation throughout fashionable circles, even in the present age of iron and steam. How much more so, then, must such a union as that which occupied the western part of London during one whole week at the period of which we speak!

The Duke de Duro and the Marchioness of Mallington, appeared to be admirably matched. The latter, as we have seen, was one of those beautiful women whose wealth and extraordinary accomplishments rendered her irresistible. No wonder, then, that a creature of passionate impulse like De Duro, should become entangled in the meshes of love.

The approaching marriage was, consequently, the theme of conversation from west to east, and from north to south. Nevertheless, it did not take place; and thus, the joy of rivals on the one hand, and admirers on the other, became once more exuberant.

Various rumours were circulated as to the] reason why the marriage had been broken off, but, as usual, few approached the truth. Some asserted that the lady alone was blameable; whilst others declared that the Duke loved another. De Duro himself declared with apparent regret, that he had failed in his suit. Some believed what he said, but a much greater number thought that he had succeeded too well. We shall see by and bye, perhaps.

At one of the evening parties of the Marchioness of Mallington, he met the Hon. Miss Littlemore, and thought that the beautiful heiress, over whose delicate features a shade of sadness had spread itself, was an almost insignificant person. A second time he met her, when Miss Littlemore sang one of her favourite airs; but her soft, weak voice, struck somewhat harshly on his ear.

He met her for the third time. It was at a concert in the saloon of Lady Elizabeth Lawson. The Duke that evening was cold and taciturn; he appeared to be absorbed in one of those dreamy fits of abstraction in which he so frequently indulged.

The Hon. Miss Littlemore, seated near her cousin, Miss Margaret Missent, in a room which had not yet been invaded by the other guests of the evening, were conversing in an under tone. Margaret was the best friend, and had been the companion in infancy, of the Hon. Henry Vernon, whom a voyage abroad had removed far from his affianced Miss Littlemore.

The two young girls appeared to be speaking of him, since they more than once pronounced his name. De Duro, leaning against a pillar in a dreamy attitude, stood, partly concealed, within hearing of the ladies.

The two young ladies, believing themselves alone, did not attempt to repress their voices, which floated in a delicious murmur towards the ears of De Duro. He, however, appeared to take no notice thereof, but seemed to enjoy the luxury of that respite which the officious attentions of a curious crowd left him.

At the moment of which we speak, however, the Duke was actually dreaming of love and marriage. His fancy pourtrayed in the distant mirror which extacy presents to the eyes of the soul, a fair young girl whose angelic look, at once tender, timid, and confiding, filled him with inexpressible delight. His face expressed a sort of enchantment, mingled with melancholy.

"Amelia! (he murmured), my sweet Amelia."

"Poor Amelia!" exclaimed Miss Margaret Missent at the same moment. She then added with a smile,—

"You are much attached to him, then?"

A profound sigh alone replied to the remark.

At the name of Amelia, De Duro suddenly opened his eyes, and he beheld with a scrutinizing glance the exquisite profile of the Hon. Miss Littlemore. The Duke, as we are aware, had twice before seen that young lady, yet, however, he fancied he now saw her for the first time. It is possible that the sweet smile which played on the lips of Miss Littlemore, had found a place in the dream that just previously took possession of the

Duke, for he suddenly felt his heart bound towards that charming girl. He regarded her with a look of ineffable joy, and mentally determined to conquer; but, being accustomed to success, did not occupy himself for a moment with adopting the means of triumphing.

Miss Littlemore did not reply to the question of her cousin for a few moments.

"I have been very sad since Harry's departure," she said at length.

The Duke now admired the delicious melody of that voice which the evening before he had thought harsh. The feebleness of its tone charmed him, because it seemed to seek an obscure corner in the tablet of his memory, and touched a chord that had reposed for years.

As he moved forward, Miss Littlemore turned round, and her pale cheek became purple. She felt convinced that their conversation had been overheard, and was again seized with the terror which the sight of the Duke had always inspired in her. She trembled from head to foot, and pressed her cousin's arm for support.

"Come," said she, leading her astonished friend towards the concert-room.

"Was there a serpent behind your chair?" demanded Miss Missent gaily.

"I don't know, but there certainly was a man close by," muttered Miss Littlemore.

Margaret turned rapidly round, and perceived the ardent gaze of the Duke de Duro as it followed the retreat of her companion. She became serious and thoughtful.

"How he gazed at her!" she murmured, with amiable solicitude, a little tinctured with envy.

Miss Littlemore trembled still more perceptibly.

"He seems bent on further conquests, (continued Margaret to herself), and probably designs to attack my friend—my cousin who is affianced. Poor Harry! I must defend the absent in such an unequal contest; and perhaps—no matter— the interest of my friends before self. Yes! I will write to him should anything occur to excite suspicion."

After the departure of the ladies, De Duro went and seated himself in the chair previously occupied by Miss Littlemore. He remained there a long time, and indulged once more in one of those waking dreams which he so much enjoyed.

"Poor Amelia (he murmured), since then, I have not loved as I do now."

And he resumed his somnolent posture in the chair.

The Duke de Duro was again in love—honestly, sincerely, irrevocably — at least so he thought. That he had been deeply smitten by the paramount attractions of the accomplished Lady Lawson it is impossible to deny—he undoubtedly loved her, yet it was but for a moment; the next erased the lively sentiment from his breast. But if any trace of that brief and passionate attachment still lingered in his memory, the approach of a more powerful and enduring one was sure to obliterate it.

A few days subsequent to the third meeting of De Duro and Miss Littlemore, the Duke was formally presented to Lord Littlemore and his sister, Lady Longton. The latter was precisely the person to appreciate all the fine qualities of the handsome Duke; she was flattered by the attentions he paid her, and foresaw that her mundane importance would be considerably augmented thereby. Indeed, Littlemore House suddenly became the centre of fashion. Every one wished to be presented there; and amongst the first to solicit that honour, were Sir Samuel Saunders, Captain Considine, Dr. Dawne, and the Chevalier Curato.

The moment they were presented at Lord Littlemore's, they surrounded Lady Longton, and each began to pay her the most assiduous court. Those four gentlemen became frequent visitors at Littlemore House, and though they were doubtless well acquainted with each other, yet no apparent imtimacy reigned between them. Nevertheless one would have supposed, especially after watching every movement closely, that they had arranged among themselves to further the interests of the Duke de Duro in every possible way.

* * * * *

After the lapse of a few weeks, an extravagant report was circulated through the length and breadth of the metropolis. It was a rumour which made the members of the clubs stare with open mouths, and spread universal alarm among the slaves of fashion.

"The Duke de Duro is going to marry, (it was said); to marry one of the most simple creatures in the kingdom! Alas! the world is coming to an end, surely."

Thus the gossips spoke, and their lamentations floated over the capital, and were re-echoed through the length and breadth of the land.

"To marry, (they argued,) was to destroy his existence, break his sceptre, tie his purse, change his poetry into the most insipid prose, and to substitute for his bright crown the cap of a fool!"

Ere that noise had become so general, the Duke de Duro had demanded the hand of the Hon. Miss Littlemore.

Contrary to his usual experience, however, the Duke had met with several obstacles, the least of which was not to be despised. At first Lady Longton, who was loyalty itself, recollecting her engagement with the Hon. Henry Vernon, absolutely refused, notwithstanding she had the strongest desire to render the Duke every assistance in her power. The reciprocal love of Harry Vernon and Miss Littlemore was the result of her labours, and she had studiously prepared their union. To abandon the interests of Harry, then, would be to undo her own work—nay more, it was direct treason to the absent, and Lady Longton was incapable of that. Secondly, Lord Littlemore, an old chivalrous nobleman, had accepted Harry, and ratified the contract with his word as a gentleman. Finally, and in the third place, Miss Littlemore loved Harry, passionately and sincerely.

Thus the Duke experienced a refusal, trebly justified by circumstances, apparently insurmountable.

But he was not the man to be discouraged, even by obstacles still more serious than those which now opposed his wishes. His long habit of success did not permit him to despair, and he knew, moreover, that with his immense power he must eventually triumph.

He called to his features a mournful look, kissed the hand of Lady Longton; and, with evident regret, precipitately retired, as one who feared he might show himself weak in the hour of misfortune.

On regaining his mansion, instead of wasting a single moment on his want of success, or concocting new plans for securing it, as some persons might expect, he mentally arranged, with the utmost *sang froid*, the details of one of the most magnificent and dazzling marriages that ever the over-excited imagination of a coquettish young girl could have dreamed of.

Lady Longton, on the contrary, was quite disconsolate. She bitterly regretted having given her interest to Harry Vernon, who, however, was a most distinguished young man, and in every way worthy of her esteem; but he was nothing in comparison with the Duke de Duro.

To add to the difficulty in which Lady Longton found herself placed, the uneasiness and melancholy of her niece appeared to increase. Her glowing representations of the Duke had made a strange impression on the generous mind of Miss Littlemore, which the latter was unable to define, but which Lady Longton deemed love.

Still, however, the image of Harry Vernon was not to be so easily effaced from the heart of his affianced. Miss Littlemore seemed to hesitate; she knew not how to escape from her embarrassment, and, possibly, did not wish to know. She sometimes made an effort to decide according to the wishes of her aunt, but found it impossible to stifle the murmurings of her own heart.

The Duke now saw that the opposition of Lord Littlemore alone remained to be overcome, but that was by no means an easy matter. In the meantime, De Duro was permitted to declare his sentiments to Miss Littlemore, who, however, during the whole of the following night, dreamed only of the Hon. Henry Vernon.

It must be admitted that the latter had chosen a very unfortunate time for travelling, but his friends had strongly persuaded him to go abroad, as much for the benefit of his health, as that of seeing the beauties of foreign countries. Harry started for Paris *en route* for the banks of the Rhine, from whence he passed through all the principal states of Europe and arrived at Rome, when a letter from his old friend Miss Messent hastened his return to England.

On arriving at his residence in London, he found two letters awaiting his perusal. The first came from the companion of his youth; and the other, dated three days previously, invited him to pass the evening at Lord Littlemore's.

A ball was announced to take place at Littlemore House the same evening that Harry Vernon had arrived in town; he, consequently, had only just sufficient time to perform his toilet before repairing thither.

—o—

CHAPTER VII.

THE BALL AT LITTLEMORE HOUSE.

IN a former chapter we described the outward characteristics of Littlemore House, and, since it is likely to become the scene of important events connected with this history, we will now proceed with a more detailed notice thereof.

Littlemore House, a seigneurial edifice situated in Park-terrace, was one of those strange palaces, erected in that doubtful style of architecture which became the order of the day in 17—. The upper windows of the principal front, overlooked the high wall of dark-brown bricks which protected it. The other side opened upon a magnificent grove, at the extremity of which extended a beautiful green, surrounded by a thick tufty shrubbery, that admirably concealed the wall which separated an excellent garden from Park-road.

The interior of Littlemore House was everything that a nobleman of princely fortune could desire.

On the evening fixed for the ball, the upper windows were brilliantly illuminated, and the two watchmen who were charged with guarding those extensive premises must have seen through the leafless branches of the trees and shrubs, the flames of innumerable lights, mellowed by the transparent draperies of the casements.

The hour fixed for the commencement of the ball at length arrived, and the magnificent saloons of Littlemore House became full by degrees. The orchestra was conducted by one of the first masters of the age; and, as dancing commenced, the rooms began to assume a truly gorgeous appearance, especially that in which Lady Longton was stationed.

Lady Longton and her niece became the centre of a numerous group, who were incessant in their salutations and compliments.

" Permit me, your ladyship, (lisped the Baron de Beaujon, raising the hand of Lady Longton to within half an inch of his lips, and making a motion as if to kiss it). Do me the favour, Mademoiselle Littlemore, to permit me. You have a most splendid fan there; indeed, I speak very seriously."

" Really, Baron, (observed Lady Longton), this is the seventh time that my niece's fan has delighted you."

The group which surrounded the two ladies, could of course do no less than laugh heartily at her ladyship's remark, since it seemed to have some designed pretensions to a sally. The Baron de Beaujon laughed longer, and, if possible, more loudly than the others.

" Admirable! (he lisped); charming! delicious!"

This time, however, the group did not laugh, which seemed to surprise the Baron, who, thus disappointed, stammered forth,—

" Indeed, I speak very seriously."

Lady Longton bowed right and left to her guests in answer to the account current of salutations; she gave her hand to Lady Elizabeth Lawson Marchioness of Mallington, and Miss Littlemore embraced her cousin at the same moment.

" Ah! Sir Samuel, (said Lady Longton to a guest who had just at the moment entered), I am delighted to see you. Pray relate to us the latest news."

" It is reported that the Duke de Duro is increasing his equipages and establishment," replied Sir S. Saunders.

" Do you speak seriously?" demanded the Baron. " It is scarcely three months since he did the same thing in Paris."

" The Duke has his reasons for doing so, doubtless," added a young lady of the group.

" But my distinguished friend De Duro has said nothing to me about it," murmured the Baron de Beaujon, whose custom it was to assume a friendly familiarity with the Duke.

" May I inquire what those reasons are?" commenced Lady Longton.

" A marriage to be sure! a marriage (responded Captain Considine); it is the leading topic of conversation to-day."

On hearing that reply, Miss Littlemore lost the faint smile which had hitherto been playing on her lip. A burning heat enveloped her head, and her hands became so cold, that Lady Longton regarded her with considerable alarm.

" How she loves him!" murmured the latter.

Miss Littlemore, however, was thinking only of Harry Vernon, whom she was no longer permitted to love, but who from morning till eve occupied her thoughts, sometimes in conjunction with the name of Duro.

The Duke, it is true, had made an impression on her mind very difficult to be explained; it was not love, yet it often partook of its symptoms. The young lady herself could scarcely, and perhaps did not care to define the sentiment with which De Duro had inspired her. As we may suppose, however, that artificial impression only attacked the mind of the young girl, but could not reach her heart. Lady Longton no longer hesitated to interpose her authoritative counsels between the affections of her niece and her intelligence; so that by dint of incessant arguments the one became blinded, and the other wrapped in an apathetic sleep.

Lady Longton perceiving the effect which that intelligence produced on her niece, was anxious to protect her from further pain, and, consequently, did not think proper to ask the name of De Duro's affianced.

" The Duke is greatly changed," remarked the Chevalier Curato.

" Do you speak seriously?" lisped the Baron.

" Indeed, it is true, (replied Captain Considine); so much so, that he can scarcely be recognised, now."

Sir S. Saunders said something analogous, and Dr. Dawne muttered one of those guttural gruntings by means of which the Germans express their approbation.

" What is the matter, then, with my dear friend?" demanded the Baron de Beaujon.

" He is in love!" replied the four gentlemen in chorus.

" Which will probably last for three or four days," added the Baron, slapping his left arm.

" For life!" remarked Captain Considine gravely.

The Hon. Miss Littlemore trembled alike with pride and anguish as she listened to those remarks; as a daughter of Eve, she could not help feeling proud, and it is extremely doubtful if one might have found throughout London a single woman who could have refrained from doing so; the anguish was a warm protestation of the heart—an awaking of stifled conscience.

The Baron de Beaujon broke out into an immoderate fit of laughter.

" Delicious! (he exclaimed.) I speak very seriously."

The ball commenced. Sir Samuel Saunders took the hand of Miss Littlemore to conduct her to the quadrille, and a general movement was perceptible throughout the rooms. A number of visitors who did not dance, assembled in a room adjoining the saloon, and Lady Longton thus found herself still surrounded by a numerous and distinguished circle.

The conversation was lively, frivolous, elegantly abusive, and not too scrupulous. Lady Longton's witty remarks afforded a rich contrast with the delectable exclamations of the Baron, and the hoarse notes of Dr. Dawne.

" Really, (observed Lady Longton with imperceptible ridicule); in the absence of the Duke, Monsieur de Beaujon is the whole soul of our reunions."

" Why should you place the Baron in the second degree of importance?" remarked a Countess.

" Really, now, (added a Baronet, somewhat satirically;) the Duke could not but be proud of the comparison."

" Ah! ladies, (stammered the Baron,) pray give me quarter—I am too great an admirer of that dear Duke to entertain such pretensions."

" No modesty, Baron; you can afford to be frank."

" Je ne le sais pas!"

" But we know, Baron, (observed Lady Longton); and you should have no reserve with us. Come, relate to us one of your amusing stories."

" Some piquant anecdote!"

" A little French gossip!"

" A bit of good slander!"

" Ah! my ladies, (lisped the Baron de Beaujon), you flatter me exceedingly—I speak seriously."

The weak and vain Baron, really believing in the sincerity of the compliments which were so profusely lavished upon him, was delighted beyond measure, at being thus appealed to.

He was a little Frenchman of about forty years of age; of an ordinary figure, and plain features. His hair crimped, and glowing with pomatum, fell over his narrow forehead in the peculiar fashion of the period. His costume had some pretension both to elegance and extravagance. To complete our description of the Baron de Beaujon, we will only add that he was fond of talking, and lisped

unmercifully; that he smiled as a man extremely vain of his peculiar attractions, and wore an enormous eye-glass, which he handled in an affected manner.

He was a nobleman of modern date, and his fortune, though by no means great, was yet amply sufficient for his purpose. He saw the almost regal perfections of the Duke de Duro, and the immense popularity of the latter turned his head. He determined to imitate the admirable bearing of that inimitable model, but knew not the utter hopelessness of the task, or the immense distance which really separated him from his prototype. In his opinion, however, De Duro was simply the eloquent speaker, the piquant talker, the elegant and handsome cavalier. All those powerful and distinguished perfections of the mind, totally escaped the enormous eye-glass of the Baron de Beaujon. But the world, which notices everything, and observes each whim or caprice through a sort of intuition as it were, quickly discovered the grotesque emulation of the poor Baron. People were highly amused by his laborious endeavours to affect the manners of the Duke, but he could not perceive it. Far from being alarmed, he redoubled his efforts, was delighted at his apparent success, and looked as great as the frog in the fable; but he did not burst, because the straps of his waistcoat prevented him from swelling beyond measure.

The turn which the conversation had now taken consequently appeared a great triumph for him. He effeminately defended himself against the eulogistic attacks of his supposed admirers, and endeavoured to recal to mind some original anecdote which had carefully been prepared for such occasions as the present.

" Come, Baron (resumed Lady Longton); modesty suits you admirably; but we are nevertheless impatient to hear one of your amusing stories. Mind, you must not exaggerate anything, not even the actions of the virtuous. I would wager a trifle that you have at this moment some enchanting anecdote to relate to us.—Listen, ladies!"

" Listen! Listen!" repeated the group.

" I would rather not relate it to-night, (commenced the Baron); I speak very seriously."

" Why not to-night?"

" Because it concerns that dear Duke de Duro."

" The Duke, did you say? Oh! relate it—relate it. Tell us quickly?" exclaimed the group.

" It is an old story, (resumed the Baron); but I only learned it to-day from a Parisian of my acquaintance. It is rather droll, I must admit; indeed, I may say it is very droll."

" Relate it, then."

" Well, then, figure to yourselves, ladies, that

during De Duro's residence in Paris, about four years ago, the Baroness d'Auv—, the Baroness de Bon—, the Countess de Car—, and the Countess de Dur— became smitten by the irresistible attractions of that dear Duke."

"No doubt! No doubt!"

"Indeed, they seemed foolishly bewildered—one might almost say they were mad with love."

"No one but the Duke could have created such a sensation," observed Curato.

"Truly, (continued the Baron); and the moment those four noble ladies discovered that the affections of each were devoted to the same object, they at once entered into a treaty offensive and defensive. Amongst other things, it was agreed that each should be at liberty to adopt her own plan of operations, but the moment that one of them had made the conquest of the Duke, the others should forthwith strike their flags, and abandon all further pretensions."

5

"And very properly too, (remarked Dr. Dawne); but proceed my dear Baron."

"The Baroness d'Auv— was extremely handsome, but very passionate and vindictive."

"You are too severe, Baron," said a young lady.

"I speak very seriously," rejoined the former.

"Pardon me, (added the young lady); but I had heard differently."

"I assure you, Mademoiselle, I do not exaggerate in the least degree. Madame d'Auv—was for taking our hero by a *coup de main*; but her designs, consequently, became too transparent to succeed. The Baroness de Bon—, who was the most amiable and timid of the four, pursued a silent and pacific course. The Countess de Car— possessed immense wealth, on which alone she confidently relied for success. Lastly, the Countess de Dui—, a woman of great spirit, wit, and beauty, was, perhaps, the most powerful of all."

"An admirable quartet;" observed Curato.

" They carried on the war with great spirit for about three weeks, (continued the Baron); at the termination of that period the battle seemed decided, for the carriage of the Countess de Dur— was observed to be stationed for four hours before the door of De Duro. The Countess de Car— could not understand how it was that her wealth should be forgotten; and the Baroness de Bon— spent a whole day in despair. The Baroness d'Auv—, however, was not to be so easily defeated; she made inquiries, and learned that her rival had succeeded in a stratagem which to some extent compromised the character of the illustrious Duke, by sending her empty coach to wait at his door."

" That was a rich idea, (remarked Captain Considine); but pray proceed, Baron."

" When the Baroness discovered that, her rage was excessive, and she determined to have her revenge; the Baroness de Bon— hastily arranged a little stratagem of her own."

" What was that ?" inquired several voices.

" She procured a miniature likeness of the Duke, and got some one to send it to her, with a letter written so much in the style of De Duro, that the Countess de Car—, to whom it was exhibited, believed it to be genuine, and reported it as such."

" Admirable !" exclaimed Dr. Dawne.

" I speak very seriously, (said de Beaujon). In the course of a day or two the trick was discovered, and the Countess de Car— resolved to demand satisfaction !"

" Such things were disgraceful, (interrupted Lady Longton). Those women dishonoured their sex."

" And their titles !" added a Baroness.

" Proceed, dear Baron, proceed, (said the Chevalier Curato); what was the result ?"

" Why, those ladies, finding each had adopted means to secure her own triumph, which were anything but fair or honourable, eventually became involved in an inextricable dispute."

" Nothing less could be expected," observed a dowager.

" Truly, (rejoined De Beaujon). Shortly afterwards, the Baroness d'Auv— accidentally encountered Madame de Dur— in the Rue de Bourbon, and observed that her conduct was disreputable."

" The matter was becoming grave," remarked Dr. Dawne.

" Indeed, I speak very seriously, (resumed the little Frenchman). The Countess de Dur— replied to the charge by an energetic tap with the fan on her opponent's cheek."

" Enough ! (exclaimed Madame d'Auv—, burning with rage); we will settle this elsewhere, if you will be good enough to refer me to a friend !"

" Bravo ! (exclaimed Captain Considine, rubbing his hands with delight); that's business ! Go on, my dear Baron."

" I speak seriously, (continued the latter;) indeed it is a grave subject. The Baroness d'Auv— replied that Madame de Car— would arrange the matter on her part."

" Very good, (observed the Countess de Dur—); I will request Madame de Bon— to wait upon her for me."

" What dragons those ladies were," said Lady Longton.

" That De Duro changes lambs into tigers," remarked Dr. Dawne.

" He does, indeed, (added Curato). So they actually fought ?"

" Wait a moment, (returned the Frenchman). After a little correspondence, those four ladies found themselves involved in an intricate and insatiable quarrel with each other ; and it was finally arranged that they should all meet together to settle their differences in a manner as extraordinary for ladies as it was chivalrous and impetuous."

" That was superb !" exclaimed Captain Considine.

" I speak very seriously, (continued de Beaujon). It was decided that they should meet at the wood of Beauvale, about noon, on a given day. The Countess de Dur— arranged the preliminaries.

" I trust, (said she on explaining the order of proceeding), that you will keep the matter a profound secret, and each come alone to the place of appointment."

" What a termagant !" observed the dowager.

" No, no, ladies; she was simply the sport of fate—that was all."

" Oh ! indeed."

" I speak very seriously. But allow me to conclude my recital. On the day after those arrangements were made, as the guard who protected the wood of Beauvale was going his rounds, he heard four reports in rapid succession, and hastened to ascertain from whence they proceeded. On arriving near the spot, he cautiously looked through the thicket, and perceived ——"

" That our four ladies had killed and eaten themselves, like the cats of Kilkenny," interrupted Captain Considine, laughing heartily.

" No, indeed. I speak very seriously, when I assert, on the contrary, that finding the first firing had been ineffectual, they prepared for a second.

" The cormorants !" exclaimed a lady.

" Tigresses !" added another.

Permit me, Mademoiselle (interrupted the Frenchman); the four ladies were standing in the form of a perfect square, at a distance of about fifteen yards between each. They had selected an admirable spot for the purpose. It was an open space near the entrance to the wood, where they found a soft carpeting in the mossy grass which grew luxuriantly about, and a clear blue sky smiling above. In the centre of the square thus formed, a small staff with the flag of De Duro was fixed; on the top of that staff, a bust of the Duke was placed with an equilibrium so nice that the slightest puff might precipitate it to the ground. Each of the combatants had one eye fixed upon the bust, and the other on her antagonist."

" Delicious!" exclaimed Signor Curato.

" I speak seriously (resumed the Baron); but listen a moment. The Baroness d'Auv— stood facing the left of the Baroness de Bon—, who in a similar manner regarded the Countess Car—; Madame de Car— was equally attentive to the Countess de Dur—; and, finally, the latter endeavoured to select a suitable spot on the left side of the Baroness d'Aur— whereon to leave her mark of 'satisfaction.' "

" Beautifully arranged!" observed Captain Considine, in a tone of admiration.

" A little longer, (said de Beaujon), and I have done. In a few minutes the bust of De Duro fell, and the next moment four reports again resounded through the wood. The Countess de Dur— slightly wounded the Baroness d'Auv, at which the other combatants were so much alarmed, that they declared themselves satisfied, and the witty Countess de Dur— was immediately proclaimed the sole candidate for the hand of the Duke de Duro."

The quadrille had just come to a conclusion, and Sir Samuel Saunders reconducted Miss Littlemore back to her place. No sooner was she seated near her aunt than the sonorous voice of a servant suddenly predominated over the thousand noises of the *fête*, and the name of the Hon. Henry Vernon issued through the saloon.

The Hon. Miss Littlemore immediately lost those delicate colours which the exercise of dancing had diffused through her features. She became fearfully pale, and placed her hand on her heart in order to calm its rapid palpitations. Lady Longton leaned towards her, and said in an undertone—

" Courage, my child, courage! and all will be right. The interview will be very embarrassing to all, but rely on me, and fear nothing. You were deceived as well as others. Besides, who knows whether Harry Vernon himself is not changed?"

The last words, which were meant for consolation, brought a tear to the eye of Miss Littlemore.

" No weakness!" resumed Lady Longton; " you no longer love him, do you?" she added with unfeigned solicitude.

Miss Littlemore did not reply.

" How could you still love him, (pursued Lady Longton,) when he has been absent so long? But the arrival of that irresistible Duke de Duro is a great misfortune for poor Harry, I must say."

Lady Longton had never been so perfectly contented with herself. She imagined that when once the dreaded interview was past, she would be able to carry out her views with regard to Miss Littlemore without interruption.

Harry Vernon was received by Lord Littlemore with a frank and hearty cordiality. His Lordship presented the young gentleman to his daughter himself; but here the scene changed. Miss Littlemore received her lover with a coldness which astonished them both. The very name of Harry had shaken her torpor, and violently torn the remaining shreds of that diabolical veil in which her free will had hitherto been partially enveloped. The sight of Harry finished that metaphysical cure. Then, by a necessary and sudden reaction, she revolted against the despotic hand which had blinded her, and for a moment caused her to doubt the purity of her sensitive heart. But she was not yet free, a fact which the presence of Lady Longton vividly reminded her of.

She cast down her eyes under Harry's earnest regards, and only replied to his compliment, pronounced in a tremulous voice, by stammering a few words destitute of point or meaning. Harry seemed perfectly crushed by a cruel apprehension. He again made an effort to speak, but at that moment Lady Longton touched him lightly on the arm with her fan.

" You have had a pleasant voyage," said she; then suddenly changing her tone, she leaned towards him and significantly observed, " Not this evening, I conjure you; people have their eyes upon her and upon us."

But Harry did not appear to understand.

" To-morrow," continued Lady Longton, in a voice in which was blended too much pity for Harry, longer to be mistaken; " To-morrow I will explain all, and believe me ever to be your friend, dear Harry; the poor girl has resisted energetically, and has suffered courageously, I assure you."

" What, my lady! (exclaimed Harry); am I to presume—"

" I entreat you, Mr. Vernon, to wait until to-morrow."

At the same time Lady Longton took Harry's hand, which she pressed with sincere cordiality. Harry silently bowed, and left overwhelmed with grief.

" Miss Littlemore has done me the honour to accept my hand for this quadrille," said Captain

Considine, as the first notes of the orchestra resounded through the room.

But Miss Littlemore remained immovable; she seemed annihilated by the conflicting interests which surrounded her.

"You will be kind enough to excuse my niece, Captain; (responded Lady Longton, who had an eye on everything); before the termination of the ball she will dance with you."

An imperceptible smile played under the dark moustache of Captain Considine.

"De Duro is very late," said he in an under tone to Dr. Dawne.

The latter replied in a low voice, and in an accent purely English, "He relies on the interest of that amiable Lady Longton, and may the devil take me if he has not good reason for doing so. Without her, I would not answer a moment for the little creature—what a timid thing it is."

"She is becoming herself again, (rejoined the Captain); I really believe she loves the other!"

"Perhaps she does. But what does that matter?"

"Nothing, as long as we have the aunt on our side!"

At that moment Lady Longton said to her niece in a low tone, "My child, the principal difficulty is accomplished; now leave the rest to me. Ah! were it not for you, my dear, I would dispense with these insipid soirees. Poor Harry! what will become of him? But your happiness is concerned, and I must think of that before every thing. Yes! I will devote myself entirely to the realization of your future welfare."

As she pronounced these words, Lady Longton imprinted a kiss on the cold forehead of her beautiful niece. "Are you ill, my love?" she inquired with affectionate solicitude.

"I know not, (murmured Miss Littlemore), but I suffer severely, and think———"

"What do you think, my child?" interrupted Lady Longton, anxiously.

"I think that we have both deceived ourselves. The sight of Harry Vernon has——"

"Is that all?" again interrupted Lady Longton, who immediately recovered her serenity; "trust to me my child; I understand these matters perfectly well. Ah! it is fortunate for you, that I have been able to read your heart."

Harry Vernon wandered about the rooms for some time, endeavouring to throw off the dreadful apprehensions which oppressed him. He had still some vague hopes, when he recollected that his reception by Lord Littlemore had been as cordial as formerly; and further, Lady Longton's words, it was true, could be interpreted in more than one sense. But Miss Littlemore! Was it possible to misunderstand that glacial coldness? Harry endeavoured to account for it, but was unsuccessful.

At length a friend stopped to press his hand and welcome him.

"What news do you bring from Rome, Harry?" inquired the friend. "But how sad you look, my dear fellow! Are you still on the sick list?"

"Ah! Harry, my boy, (exclaimed another,) how are you? Why, how melancholy you look! Are you aware of it already?"

"What?" demanded Harry with anxiety.

"Poor fellow! (muttered the friend,) I am sorry I spoke; there is nothing but report as yet."

"To what do those reports allude?" inquired Harry, hastily.

"They say—but in all probability it is not true——"

"No matter (interrupted Harry, impatiently); tell me, I beseech you."

"Well then," resumed the friend, reluctantly, "it is said that Miss Littlemore is about to be united to the Duke de Duro."

Harry passed his hand over his forehead, and staggered towards a seat. The next moment he bounded forward in a state of bewildered excitement, bordering on madness.

"Who is this De Duro?" he imperiously demanded.

His friend regarded him with a sort of stupefaction.

"Have you not yet heard of him, then?"

"No!" replied Harry, abruptly.

"Of whom do they speak on the continent? De Duro is a Duke and a Prince, if not more; there is not his equal in England, France, or Spain. Ah! yonder is Sir Samuel, who desires to speak with me—good night, my dear friend."

Harry remained alone, completely overwhelmed by what he had just heard.

"Ah! *Bon jour, mon cher ami!* (exclaimed a shrill voice in his ear.) It is an age since I saw you last! And I was saying yesterday—let me see, what did I say? Yes, I said yesterday—But to whom did I say that? Ah, I mentioned it to that dear Duke de Duro."

"The devil!" exclaimed Harry involuntarily.

"No, my dear fellow, it was not the devil—I speak very seriously when I say that De Duro is not the king of darkness, but the king of—of—of fashion. Well, sir, I said to that distinguished personage—it is an age since Harry Vernon has been seen. But you have an air of chagrin—what am I thinking of? Why I have been told that De Duro—"

"It is perfectly true then?" interrupted Harry.

" I know nothing about it, my dear fellow. The fact is, that dear Duro conducts his affairs with the art of a necromancer, and it is not easy to see the object of his designs."

The Baron de Beaujon then turned round, and went to chatter elsewhere.

Harry again walked about in the vain endeavour to calm his agitated feelings. At length he seated himself in an obscure recess, and at the same moment felt the hand of a woman touch his own.

" Mr. Henry Vernon, (said the Marchioness of Mallington); you seem unhappy, and I believe you have cause for being so. You are doubtless aware that——"

" I believe I know all!" interrupted Harry with a profound sigh.

" All! no, Mr. Vernon, not quite; but listen a moment. The same hand which strikes you also falls heavily on me! I suffer dreadfully, and wish to assuage your pain as far as I am able, in the hope that I may thereby mitigate my own. There appears to be a demon of fatuity at the bottom of every man's heart."

Absorbed by the contemplation of his painful position, Harry did not appear to understand clearly the consolatory observations which had just been addressed to him. He consequently regarded the Marchioness of Mallington with an astonished air. A smile of sadness overspread the countenance of the latter.

" I shall probably be enabled to furnish you with the means of combatting De Duro, (she pursued); but one cannot vanquish that all-powerful individual with ordinary arms."

" De Duro again! always De Duro!" thought Harry, who felt a boundless and maddening hatred arise in his heart.

" Come and see me to-morrow," continued the Marchioness of Mallington.

" To-morrow!" murmured Harry.

" Yes! I wish to speak to you of matters which can only be mentioned in whispers and closed doors; in a room, too, where none but ourselves will be present. Even then our secrets may become known to an enemy who is as unscrupulous as powerful. To-morrow, then, to-morrow I shall expect you, Mr. Vernon."

She bowed gracefully, and smiled as though she had just concluded a frivolous conversation. But Harry Vernon had not so much influence over himself; his distress was clearly depicted on his features, and he sat the very image of despair. His cousin, Miss Mary Missent, at length perceived him, and hastened to take up a position by his side.

" I have been looking anxiously for you," observed Harry, heaving a deep sigh.

" And I also sought you (said Miss Missent), for I have much to say.—Did you get my letter?

" Yes, but why were you not more explicit? I should then have hastened home and prevented this misfortune."

" Impossible, I fear, Harry; but the fact is, I knew nothing certain. Indeed, I only suspected the approach of that blow which has so cruelly stricken you."

" You are our mutual friend, (murmured Harry, after a brief silence); and must therefore know the real sentiments of her heart. I beseech you, then, to tell me——"

" I will tell you all I know, (interrupted Miss Missent); but you must summon all your courage, my dear cousin."

" Speak of her, Mary; I am impatient to know what she thinks of it."

" Believe me, Harry, she suffers as much as you. There is something strange in her demeanour which I cannot exactly comprehend, but I am perfectly convinced that her heart has not changed. You may rest assured that Miss Littlemore still loves you."

A smile of happiness momentarily rested on the handsome features of the young man.

" But that marriage?"

" It is spoken of, and that is all as yet, though Lady Longton desires it, I believe, and Miss Littlemore submits to her wishes."

" She submits?" repeated Harry mournfully.

" De Duro has bewitched them, I verily believe,"

" Still De Duro! (muttered Harry,) Do you know this De Duro, Mary?"

" I do not know him," replied Miss Missent, looking down and blushing.

" I fear he has also bewitched you, my cousin, (remarked Harry Vernon in a tone of regret). Will you point him out to me, Mary? But first tell me what he is?"

" He is a being whom no one can resist," responded the young girl in an under tone.

" Indeed! (exclaimed Harry,) but we shall see that by and bye perhaps."

" He is a magnificent cavalier, Harry—both noble and powerful, one whose mighty influence throws other men into utter insignificance! Woe to his rivals!"

" Woe to him, rather!" interrupted Vernon, who rose in a moment of passionate excitement. " Show him to me, I tell you! I must instantly see that man face to face! I must and will confront him! Shew him to me, I beseech you."

At that moment a sonorous voice resounded

through the saloon, and interrupted Harry, announcing :—

"Don Juan-Maria - Dio-Monti-Figuelles-Marco d'Allicant, Prince Duke of Duro !"

The name thus pompously pronounced, reached the burning ear of Harry Vernon just at the moment when he was calling out for his rival, when fate suddenly threw him in his face. Harry, trembling with rage, and galvanised by that ferocious joy which heroic persons assume at the approach of an enemy, suddenly shook off his torpor, and precipitately dashed through the crowd.

He instinctively stopped half way between the door and that part of the saloon which was occupied by Lady Longton and her niece ; naturally supposing that De Duro must come that way, he placed himself in readiness to receive him.

The Duke appeared immediately after. He was a man of tall stature, and noble bearing; his fine, and rather delicate features partook of that distinctive expression which forms the chief characteristics of the Spaniard, but in a moderate degree. He was superlatively handsome; and wore a slight moustache, black as jet, in the fashion of the Spanish and the Portuguese. His fine hair, naturally curly, fell in rich waves over his high forehead, replete with candour and pride.

The Duke's step was regal and majestic. He wore a costume of supreme elegance, and four sovereign orders sparkled on his breast, besides other marks of minor distinction.

The moment his name was pronounced, a suppressed murmur ran through the throng, indeed such was the excitement it caused, that many of the ladies made false movements in the quadrilles ; others forgot to reply to the momentary observations of their partners; and several stood still in the midst of the dance. There was another element in that brilliant *fête*, and each fair one felt her instinct of coquetry increase with unusual rapidity.

Poor Harry Vernon! He was scarcely thought of in the presence of the illustrious Duke; but he could not, in fact, be compared with that magnificent personage. Harry was undoubtedly handsome, but his beauty did not consist so much in the regularity of his features, as in the pleasing reflection of his generous disposition, which brightened up his noble forehead. There was something in his physiognomy extremely chivalric. He was affable, courteous, and engaging; in a word, he would have been the lion of that brilliant assemblage, had not the Duke de Duro deprived him of that distinction.

Harry was much younger than the Duke, although the latter was one of those singular men on whom age leaves no traces, and whom time in its rapid course seemed to forget. It was impossible to say, precisely, how many summers had illumined the shining brow of De Duro. Still, however, one no longer perceived that flower of youth, which the good-humoured features of Harry Vernon presented.

The young man steadfastly and haughtily regarded the motions of his triumphant rival, who slowly passed through the narrow passage which the throng opened for him. At the first glance, it seemed to Harry that he had somewhere seen the advancing figure, though under such unfavourable circumstances, that the impression it made on his mind was extremely furtive, and he could only remark with extreme jealousy the extraordinary beauty of De Duro. His hatred became almost ungovernable, and added to that alarm which pressed so heavily on his wounded soul.

Continuing to regard his rival with a look of defiance, Harry Vernon moved forward with the view to obstruct his passage, but the Duke, who did not perceive this, suddenly paused, and sought with his eye Lady Longton and her niece.

"Below there! below, my Lord Duke," exclaimed the officious Baron de Beaujon, pointing at the same time to that part of the saloon where those ladies were seated. "The ladies have been complaining of your late arrival. Come, Vernon, my dear fellow, have the goodness to make way for the Duke and me."

Harry did not move an inch; but his eyes, which were still fixed on the Duke, expressed the most provoking contempt. Duro regarded him calmly for a moment, and then replied to the mute defiance of his young rival, by a salutation replete with courtesy.

"I will endeavour to have the honour of being presented to Mr. Harry Vernon, presently," said he mildly.

"I shall be most happy to introduce you," commenced the Baron de Beaujon; but he was stopped short by the threatening looks of the young man, who abruptly exclaimed,—

"Enough!"

"I speak very seriously," faltered de Beaujon.

The Duke regarded Harry with a serene smile; then, turning towards a gentleman who had followed him into the saloon, made an imperceptible, but significant sign with his head, and proceeded in a different direction to that which he had apparently intended.

The individual who had taken his place, and on whose approach every one made way, was elegantly attired; but the superb ball dress which decorated his person scarcely concealed that insignificant and citizen-like appearance with which nature had endowed him. With an exalted head, and eyes wide open, he marched forward, apparently indifferent to everything that was passing around him.

"And who is that singular personage?" mentally exclaimed a guest of the evening. It was the blind man of the "Thames Tap."

At the moment when Duro disappeared among the guests, the blind man stepped forward and placed himself before Harry, by which means the latter lost sight of his rival.

"Be so good as to stand aside, sir," said Vernon, in an angry tone.

With his motionless and death-like eyes, the blind man turned towards him an inquiring glance.

"Did you address me?" he mildly demanded.

"Yes, sir! and I deem it very strange——"

"There, there, my dear fellow," interrupted Beaujon, bursting into a loud laugh; "what is the matter with you this evening? Are ye about to seek a quarrel with Sir Samuel Seelie, who is blind?"

"I ask your pardon, sir," murmured Harry, biting his lips with vexation. He then sought the Duke with his eyes, but without success, whilst the blind man replied,—

"It is I, sir, who should ask pardon for my awkwardness."

Harry still continued to look about for his rival. He deemed it strange that the Duke should have, seized with so much eagerness the opportunity which chance had appeared to offer him for escape.

"Can he be a coward?" murmured Harry. Perhaps that is the real cause why he avoided one. But it would be much better for me if he were brave!"

"You will find, then, that he is just what you wish, young gentleman!" observed a railing voice in his ear.

Harry turned quickly round, but there was no one near him except a tall personage, with a foreign appearance, who was laboriously wiping his eye-glass.

"What did you say?" inquired the young man imperiously.

"I did not speak," phlegmatically replied the tall personage, who was no other than our worthy acquaintance, Dr. Dawne.

"You addressed me, sir."

"You are mistaken," replied the German, turning on his heel.

Harry thought he really must have been deceived; and yet he had heard distinctly enough. His ears tingled, and he became feverish with excitement.

Just at that moment the Duke had joined Lady Longton and her niece. The spot where they were seated suddenly became the centre of attraction; every glance was turned in that direction, and the group which surrounded her ladyship was instantly doubled. The latter received her distinguished guest as a parent receives a favourite and admired son.

"My niece has become quite melancholy," said she, while Duro kissed the young girl's hand.

"Was it my absence which caused Miss Littlemore's sadness?" demanded the Duke, with a smile.

The young girl endeavoured to smile too, but found it impossible. Her misery became more complicated by the presence of the Duke, who had not in the slightest degree lost that mysterious influence which he had exercised over her; although the sudden arrival of Harry Vernon, her affianced, might, under ordinary circumstances, have had that effect. But the Duke de Duro, as we have shown, exercised a power by no means of an ordinary nature; on the contrary, his pleasure triumphed against everything, and no woman attempted to oppose his advances.

That evening, too, De Duro was infinitely more amiable and eloquent than usual. He had resolved, not merely to conquer, but to render all idea of rivalry impossible. When, therefore, the inexperienced Miss Littlemore found herself overwhelmed by the earnest attentions of the Duke, she could scarcely avoid abandoning herself to the enchantment of the moment, notwithstanding an inward voice whispered in her ear the name of one whom she really loved. The soothing words of De Duro, however, sank deep in her breast, and produced a powerful impression—it was something more than fascination; in fact, Miss Missent had correctly defined it when she said that her cousin was "bewitched!"

Harry Vernon remained standing in a thoughtful attitude. He was at too great a distance from the group to hear anything they said; but the moment he awoke from his lethargy, observed all, and drank with poignant avidity the bitter cup of jealousy to its dregs. He gazed with strained eyes and beating heart on the happy group which surrounded his affianced; and it seemed as if his entire soul was in arms—interrupting each gesture, giving to every movement a signification, which added to his fever and redoubled his sufferings. When De Duro leaned towards Amelia, and entranced her with all the magic of his look, Harry thought he read therein a silent but eloquent love, and his rage was turned to excruciating agony.

Hours passed, during which one thing only occurred to diversify the tormenting espionage of poor Harry. At the moment when the conversation of the group which surrounded Lady Longton had attained its highest degree of animation, De Duro, carried away, doubtless, by the heat of the argument, frowned for an instant. The light of a chandelier fell directly on his animated countenance, and vividly depicted that scowl. Harry, who was steadfastly gazing on him at the moment, trembled involuntarily, and asked himself for the second time, where he had previously seen that man. But the Duke's features immediately resumed their normal position, and Harry was again doubtful. The reminiscence which at that moment traversed his mind, referred to an event so terrible, and his memory recalled a picture so hideous—whether real or imaginary, that jealousy and hatred, however intense, were not sufficient to connect De Duro with its perpetration. Harry felt he must be deceived—that a person with the serene and noble bearing of the Duke, was incapable of such a crime as that which his memory recalled at the moment.

Harry, consequently, resigned his whole soul to vengeance. His anger could not be mistaken, it was concentrated on the Duke, leaving Amelia, (whose comparatively feeble and subdued character he well knew), entirely out of the question.

At length De Duro rose, and proceeded to pay his respects to the ladies assembled. Harry, who had been impatiently awaiting that moment, quitted his post, and hastened to meet him.

"My lord!" said he, with that affected calmness which the man of the world always knows how to cast over his most poignant emotions; "you just now manifested the desire of being presented to me, I believe?"

De Duro did not appear to recognise him.

"You expressed a wish of being presented to me?" repeated Harry with marked emphasis.

The Duke smiled significantly, and extended his hand towards Harry.

"Mr. Vernon," said he, "I indeed have a sincere desire to form an acquaintance with a gentleman of whom Lady Longton has so often spoken with the affection of a mother, and whom Miss Littlemore loves as a cherished brother."

"Perhaps you, too, are loved as a ' cherished brother?'" said he with a bitter smile.

De Duro did not withdraw his hand.

"Not exactly," he replied significantly.

"I understand," resumed Harry, whose wrathful indignation was becoming insupportable; "you are playing a fine game!"

"Sir!" said the Duke with ineffable mildness.

"I repeat, my lord," continued Harry with increasing warmth "you are playing a fine trick."

"Nay, sir," commenced De Duro, with a bland smile.

"You *are*, my Lord Duke," interrupted Harry vehemently; "and I find myself falling into the ridiculous position of a forgotten lover, who annoys everybody by his presence, and whom every one holds either in contempt or pity! My lord, I beg to inform you that I love Miss Littlemore!"

An affable smile still played on the noble features of the Duke.

"I know it," he replied in a cold tone, but with exquisite moderation; "Lady Longton has already made me acquainted with the fact. But I hoped—indeed we all hoped that absence—"

"Of whom do you speak, my lord?" interrupted Harry, with impatience.

"I speak of myself and Lady Longton;" replied the Duke in a mild tone.

"Indeed!" again interrupted Harry, in an imperious voice. "If you pronounce another name I shall declare that you are a liar!"

The Duke still smiled, and with exquisite modulation, added—

"As also the Honourable Miss Amelia Littlemore!"

"Enough, my Lord! Enough!" exclaimed Harry, who at the same time placed his fingers on his lips, with apparent gratification.

"Mr. Vernon," said the Duke, mildly, "I could have wished for your friendship, but you have decided otherwise. Be it so!"

Harry blushed with pleasure, and felt gratified to think he should have his revenge.

"To-morrow, then," he whispered.

"Agreed!"

"At break of day."

"I am already prepared!"

"It is my determination that one of us should die!" said Harry firmly.

"I NEVER LEAVE AN ENEMY ALIVE!"

As he uttered these significant words, De Duro replied to the astonished gaze of his rival by a frown so terrible, that the latter seemed almost annihilated. He staggered to a seat, and the moment he had partially recovered himself, muttered in a tremulous voice, "That face again! It is the devil himself!"

—o—

CHAPTER VIII.
MARY.

The card which blind Bolton had given to the beautiful girl of the Thames Tap, by the river side, as related in a previous chapter, bore on its shining surface the following inscription:—

No. 3,
Warwick Terrace,
Park Place.

Punctually at the hour appointed Mary arrived,

passed through the large iron gateway, ascended the stone steps, and rapped at the door of that house, according to the instructions she had previously received in Lower Thames Street.

It was really a splendid mansion, and so thought Mary, who found it unnecessary to knock more than once; for the moment that the sound re-echoed through the hall, the door was opened. A domestic in splendid livery received her without uttering a word, and preceded her into the first apartment on the ground floor, where a lady-like person appeared to be awaiting her arrival.

On the entrance of Mary, the latter personage precipitately arose, and, dropping a curtsey as graceful and prolonged as ever any theatrical artist could have performed, observed,—

"I have the honour to announce the arrival of Her Highness the Princess to the Duchess of Durillo. Will your Highness deign to enter the saloon? Or perhaps you would prefer ascending to your apartment previously to doing so? Your Highness is now at home."

The poor young girl regarded the speaker with a look of mingled pride and astonishment. She could not help contrasting the tone and language of the person who now addressed her, with that of the vulgar Mrs. Mouthy, and felt both gratified and embarrassed at the sudden change in her prospects. Recollecting that she had already been informed that house was henceforth to be hers, she replied—

"I am aware of it."

She was then escorted into a very beautiful apartment, luxuriantly furnished in the richest style of the period. She threw herself into an arm-chair, and her attendant, who had been appointed her lady's maid, retired, making a low curtsey.

The beautiful girl of the dirty tavern, who had thus unexpectedly been addressed in such respectful terms, began to muse on her improved fortune.

She had exchanged her old costume for one of an elegant, fantastic, and almost of a theatrical pattern. A black velvet dress admirably pourtrayed her magnificent figure; and instead of a bonnet, she wore an enormous lace veil carelessly thrown over her head.

In the bright sun of day, as well as by the sparkling lustres of the night, she was exquisitely beautiful; but one might now perceive in the proud repose of her enchanting features, a something very nearly approaching to fatigue. It was the result of that suffering and anguish which she had endured during the preceding week. In the day-time, however, there was less vigour and real courage in the physiognomy of that marvellous creature, than in the more feeble light of the night.

Her elbow was supported on the sculptured arm of the chair, and her head rested on her hand. For several minutes she sat in an attitude of profound reflection, without bestowing a single glance on the magnificent furniture of the apartment into which she had thus suddenly been shown.

Presently a door of the apartment turned softly on its hinges, whilst the hangings which covered it were drawn aside. At the threshold stood the figure of an old lady, who seemed almost lost in a multiplicity of ribbons and lace. She was short and thin, and appeared anxious to hide her increasing years in the exuberent dress which enveloped her person. Two piercing eyes glittered beneath her agitated and trembling eyelashes; and her features appeared cold and nerveless.

She stopped at the entrance and directed her glances towards the young girl; then gazed on her for some time, and when she had concluded her examination, a smile and murmur of satisfaction escaped her.

"Perfect!" mentally exclaimed the old lady; "she is indeed perfect! Oh! give me a blind man like Bolton to discover the beauties of the capital."

She then closed the door behind her, and approached the meditative Mary. The latter, hearing a step, slowly turned round.

"My dear girl," said the old lady; "I am the Duchess Dowager of Durillo, in Spain. You will henceforth be my child — the widow of my unfortunate Antonio, who died in the blossom of his age, to the great grief of all. Yes! hence-forward you will be the Princess Mary de Seville! Come and embrace me, my dear child."

The old lady then imprinted a hearty kiss on the forehead of her newly adopted daughter.

"Princess!" exclaimed Mary, in a tone of wonder mingled with delight.

"Yes!" replied the Duchess; "the Princess Mary of Seville! You will recollect the name I trust. It is that of the beloved husband whom you have lamented for the last six months."

"Princess Mary!" murmured the young tavern girl.

"Certainly, my little beauty! the Prin-cess Ma-ry—de—Se-ville!" again repeated the Duchess, emphasising each syllable. "You will not forget it, I trust?"

"Oh, no," replied Mary, as she fixed her fine sparkling eyes, replete with affectionate interest, on the smiling countenance of her new parent; "it may as well be Seville as anything else for aught I know or care."

"Fie Princess! Fie upon thee, child. What, no more respect than that for the descendant of such an illustrious name as Munoz? We, who have royal blood flowing in our veins, though not, perhaps, of the most pure quality, are accustomed to receive the utmost deference and homage. Indeed, more than an hundred poets have sung, and historians recorded the brilliant fame of our noble ancestors."

The old lady delivered this little speech with an emphasis partly serious and partly humorous.

"Princess," she continued, seating herself in an arm chair near that of the handsome Mary; "you are now my daughter, and I am your parent; we must, consequently, appear much attached to each other for the future; the law of nature is formal in that respect. You are, indeed, the most beautiful girl I have met with for the last sixty years; but I need not have mentioned that, for you have doubt-less already been made acquainted with the fact. By the bye, here are your arms, my dear child, this will henceforth be your signet."

As she pronounced the last word, the Duchess placed a large ring encircled with brilliants, on the finger of the blushing Mary. It bore quarterly with those of the Munoz family, the arms of Spain.

"Let us now speak of business," she resumed. "In the first place, oblige me by reading this letter, which is addressed to you."

The young girl took the letter, opened it with some hesitation, and read as follows,—

London, ——.

"Mademoiselle,

"The moment you accepted the assistance of the blind man in Lower Thames Street, it was un-reservedly rendered; when you acceded to his proposition, you at once became united to a society as powerful as it is mysterious and energetic. As a new member of this mighty association, it be-came necessary to know how you were disposed to act, hence it was seen that on leaving the man who saved your life, you proceeded to St. Martin's-in-the-Fields, where you walked several times round the ruins of a large mansion—"

"That house was my father's!" murmured Mary.

"After which you returned along the Strand, through Fleet Street, up Ludgate Hill, and entered a carriage in Cheapside; you desired the coachman to drive you to the Arlington Arms in Mint Street, where you passed the first night. On the following morning you arose at an early hour, and left on foot. The first place you visited was a retired coffee-house in Abdale Street, where you breakfasted on three slices of bread and butter and an egg, with one cup each of coffee and chocolate—"

"That is true!" interrupted Mary, with surprise, and she again resumed the perusal of the letter.

"You next proceeded to a clothes-warehouse, where you purchased, for three guineas and a half, that fantastic costume which must forthwith be exchanged for one more becoming. After that, you went to the corner of Hampton Street, and waited there three hours and five minutes for a person who did not come—"

"Who did not come!" repeated Mary in a musing tone.

"You were extremely anxious to see him, nevertheless," continued the letter, which seemed to respond to the interruption of the young girl. "You left Hampton Street, but soon returned; again you left, and returned once more. Finally, after waiting for another hour, you went back to the coffee-house where you had breakfasted, and remained there during the rest of the week. Thus, you see, nothing is concealed from the eye which is henceforth open to all your actions! Be faithful, patient, and discreet! When your instructions arrive, obey them implicitly, and be silent! By this means you will acquire advantages which none but those connected with this all-powerful association could ever boast of."

When she had concluded the perusal of that letter, to which there was no signature, the young girl refolded it and regarded her new parent with a smile, which seemed to say, "Very good, I understand."

"You have read the letter, my dear?" observed the Duchess.

"Yes;" replied Mary, with an imperceptible frown. "I have been followed, it seems."

"I cannot exactly deny it," rejoined the old lady; "at the same time I think you must be mistaken."

"Impossible!" exclaimed Mary, "why they have observed everything—even the most minute

circumstance that has occurred to me during the past week."

"That is not surprising, my child."

"Not surprising?"

"The association—"

"Is very strong," interrupted Mary abruptly; "I know it. But they have menaced me in this letter, a proceeding which I do not like. It is preposterous to threaten a young girl whom they found on the road to death."

The piercing eyes of the Duchess Dowager of Durillo fell beneath the scrutinizing glance of her adopted daughter, like the horns of a snail when in contact with a rougher substance; she thus found herself unexpectedly subdued, and for some time observed a profound silence.

"Pardon me, my dear child," said she at length in a tone slightly submissive, and perfectly free from that raillery which was remarkable in her first words; "you are going much too far, my dear. If you have been followed, it is through pure solicitude for the welfare of that society of which you are now a member. They call themselves powerful, and well indeed they might, for their power extends to a degree which it is impossible to conceive. With regard to menaces, I take upon myself to affirm that you are mistaken. They never menace: they strike! You will be of immense service to them in the accomplishment of a grand project, perchance of many—that depends on yourself. But in exchange, you will receive power, luxury, pleasure, and happiness unlimited."

"Happiness!" murmured Mary, whose eyes brightened up at the thought, "Alas! how can I be happy when he does not love me?"

"Who is it that does not love thee my child?"

"He does not even know me," continued Mary, sighing.

"So much the better."

The beautiful girl of the Thames Tap, or rather the Princess Mary of Seville, as we should now designate her, perhaps, regarded the Duchess with a look of anxious inquiry.

"I do not understand you," said she.

"He does not know you?"

"No!"

"Then how can he love one with whom he is not even acquainted?"

"That is very true! It did not strike me before."

"Because love had obscured your perceptive faculties."

A profound sigh escaped the young girl, whose eyes were bent upon the floor.

"Are you aware how much more seductive you

have become since the meeting in Lower Thames Street?" observed the old lady. "Then you were only pretty, to-day you are superlatively beautiful; henceforth you will be rich, titled, and august—in fact, perfectly irresistible! According to the fidility with which you serve the mysterious power of which we were just now speaking, so will that power serve you. From this moment you form one of the countless links which compose the mighty chain that binds this inscrutable society together. You will add to its immense strength, and thereby acquire a power yourself, which an ordinary member of society dare not hope for. Whatever you wish will be accomplished! That which might hitherto have appeared impossible, will become simple, and easily acquired!"

The beautiful girl raised her eyes, and regarded the old lady with an astonished gaze as she concluded those strange remarks.

"Can you work miracles?" inquired Mary, with a pleasing but incredulous smile.

"What do you require, my child?"

"A miracle!" repeated Mary.

"Let me hear it."

"I desire reciprocal love! can you ensure me that?"

The old lady drew her adopted daughter to her breast, and with a benignant smile replied,—

"Yes! it is possible, I have no doubt."

"You will, then?" exclaimed Mary, with inexpressible delight. She raised her eyes towards the ceiling, and two tears slowly descended her blooming cheeks.

"Yes, my dear. But you have been weeping, have you not?"

"Oh, yes, a great deal," replied Mary.

"You will now forget what tears are."

"Alas! I doubt it; since the man I love so much regards me with indifference."

"He is doubtless very rich and powerful?" observed the Dowager Duchess of Durillo.

"On the contrary, I believe he is extremely poor. He used to come and borrow money of my father, before we left the house in St. Martin's Fields, which is now demolished."

"What is the gentleman's name?"

"Victor Vernon," replied the beautiful girl, with a gesture of pride.

"Victor Vernon!" repeated the old lady with surprise; "the poor Viscount who has lately married a rich heiress?"

"Married!" exclaimed Mary.

"Yes! But be not alarmed, my child, for if it be the Viscount Vernon who has caused your uneasiness there is nothing to fear—"

"But he is united to another you say?" interrupted Mary in an anxious tone.

"That is true," replied the Duchess. "The bride, however, was barbarously assassinated on the day of marriage, and the young Viscount is again free."

"Free!" echoed the beautiful girl, with the deepest emotion. "There is hope, then?"

"Nay, more than hope, for you love him exceedingly, I perceive."

"I am proud to love him!"

"You are right, my beauty," rejoined the Duchess. And it was he whom you sought at the corner of Hampton Street, I presume?"

The young girl made an affirmative sign with her head.

"My poor dear child," resumed the old lady; "had he passed, it is probable that he would not have observed you; had he not noticed you then, the consequences would have been serious. Do not open your fine eyes so widely, my child; you may rely upon it that the Viscount Vernon does not fall in love with young ladies whom he meets by chance at the corners of streets."

"True!" murmured Mary, resuming her meditative attitude.

"The Princess Mary of Seville must not meet her friends thus, but at the brilliant re-unions of fashionable life; at the theatre, or behind the windows of an emblazoned equipage, as she drives through the parks."

"Yes, I had forgotten that they promised me luxuries and riches."

The young girl immediately arose and gazed round the apartment, as though she had suddenly become aware of the reality of her altered position. She surveyed the sumptuous furniture of the saloon with inexpressible delight, and a smile of gratification illumined her exquisitely modelled features.

"Ah!" exclaimed Mary, joyfully; "this reminds me of the beautiful house in St. Martin's Fields, which is now in ruins. Oh! I could live here as I formerly did at my father's before he was—was—was—"

"Hanged!" whispered the old lady soothingly; "it is a dreadful word, my poor child, for a daughter to pronounce."

"You are aware of it, then?" observed Mary with a mixture of surprise and regret.

"We know all, my dear; you need not, therefore, have any reserve with me. Let us, however, converse on a more agreeable and appropriate subject. You are now at home, in a mansion suitable to your great merits, and where, I trust, you will be supremely happy."

"I hope so," rejoined Mary with a sigh. "I shall amuse my spare moments as formerly. Yes, I will paint, sing, and read; and sometimes I shall see Lord Vernon."

The young girl smiled serenely as she pronounced the loved name, and, after a moment's pause, turned suddenly towards the Duchess, who was regarding her with a look of admiration.

"When shall I see him?" she inquired.

The old lady reflected a moment, crossing her small attenuated hands over her knees, and partially closing each eye.

"You shall see him this evening," she at length replied.

"This evening!" exclaimed Mary, with inexpressible delight; "this evening! do you really mean this evening?"

"Yes!"

"Is it possible!" continued the young girl in a state of delirium.

"With us all things human are possible!"

"And I shall really see him?"

"Without fail!"

Then resuming her graceful attitude, she extended her hands towards the old lady, and said, with an expression of infinite gratitude,

"Thanks, ten thousand thanks; I shall now love you as a mother."

The old lady slowly shook her head, and then observed,—

"My poor child, you are indeed most passionately fond of him; but such attachment as yours is extremely dangerous, because it will exclude prudence."

"How so?"

"Will you be able to keep secrets from him, for instance?"

"Certainly not!" replied Mary, emphatically, "I shall tell him everything."

"Nay, that must not be; one word and you are lost!"

"What matters?"

"*You will also kill him!*"

The sweet smile which had recently shone over the exquisite features of that enchanting girl, was instantly replaced by a stern frown.

"I am not threatening you, my dear child," mildly resumed the old lady; "your angry looks are therefore superfluous. I know as well as any one the impulsive character of the Viscount Vernon, and, consequently, wish to guard against the consequences of any indiscretion. Should you utter but one word he would guess the rest, and, consequently attempt to thwart our views, if not agreeable to him. Now TO CONTEND AGAINST US IS TO RUSH INTO CERTAIN DEATH! He is but one, while the association is so multitudinous, that it can no longer count its numbers. He is weak, but

we are all-powerful! He is the heir to an empty title—a simple gentleman; whereas we have amongst us persons of every grade, from the greatest duke to the weakest mendicant. In short, our society is superlatively influential, numerous, and terrible! If he were to attempt opposition the first shock would completely annihilate him!"

"I will be silent," interrupted Mary.

"I believe you, my child," pursued the Duchess, casting a profound and scrutinizing look on her adopted daughter. "You will be taciturn for his sake, for you know that *there are eyes which see, and ears that are open all around*. As the Princess Mary of Seville, you will know how to enjoy present happiness, and not engage in an absurd and insane struggle. You may give the Viscount your love, and is not that sufficient? The love of a Princess, twenty years of age, more beautiful than an angel, and richer than a queen!"

"It is scarcely sufficient, for the Viscount is very much superior to all others; but I will remain quiet for his sake. You told me I should see him this evening?"

"And so you shall, my child."

The Duchess rose and rang the bell. Two seconds afterwards the lady's-maid appeared, and in obedience to an order to that effect, brought the materials for writing.

"It is now three o'clock," muttered the Duchess Dowager, tracing a few words on the paper; "we have three hours yet, and that is more than we require. Give this letter to Robert, Mary Ann, and desire him to take it to the Doctor with all possible speed. Give this one to James; it is necessary that the Major should have this within half an hour. Desire William, moreover, to get the Princess's carriage ready for half-past six o'clock."

The lady's maid departed.

"My dear child," resumed the Duchess, "there is a new piece to be performed at the King's Theatre this evening. It is something more than ordinary, I believe, and likely to be fashionably attended. Commence your toilet, my beauty; Mary Ann awaits your pleasure. We will go to the theatre this evening."

"And Vernon?"

"The Viscount Vernon will be there, my dear."

"How do you know that?"

"By means of our association!"

"Does he attend the theatres regularly?"

"By no means."

"Then why to night?"

"To meet you, my child!"

"To meet me!" replied Mary, with the utmost astonishment and delight.

"Yes! Do you not desire to see him?"

" Undoubtedly; but how is it that he attends to-night in order to meet me?"

" Because the Supreme Head of our association desires to gratify your wishes!"

" May I ask who this wonderful being is that wields such extraordinary power?"

" HE IS THE KING OF THE MENDICANTS!"

—o—

CHAPTER IX.

THE MERCANTILE TRANSACTIONS OF ARMSTRONG AND CO. EXCITE AN EXTRAORDINARY SENSATION.

In the year of grace One Thousand Seven Hundred and odd, there was, a little beyond the angle formed by the junction of Moor-lane with Upper Thames-street, a narrow and sombre thoroughfare called Mint-lane. About the middle of the latter street stood a large, high house, with an obscure front, and narrow windows with small panes.

Few persons were observed in this lane except those whose residence or occupation led them into it. As the night approached, the lower casements of the houses exhibited their bright lights, and clamours incessantly emanated from neighbouring taverns. From thence one frequently heard the pleasant sound of money ringing on the counters, and joyous songs, abruptly terminated by the hoarse maledictions of popular quarrels.

None of those excellent qualities which constitute the amiable cut-throat and accomplished brigand, were wanting in the choice circles of that gloomy neighbourhood. Poor, in the midst of riches; dark and sombre, too, in the immediate vicinity of streets that were brilliantly lighted up; there was not even wanting the proximity of a watch-box—that admirable protection for suspicious retreats.

The greater portion of the ground floor of the large mysterious house consisted of two warehouses of equal size. The first exhibited behind the diamond panes of its casement a truly magnificent assortment of jewellery. The latter contained the various objects which constitute the toilette of both sexes, from the superb robes of the nobility, to the coarse coverings of the mendicants. These two warehouses did wonders in the way of business. Over the jeweller's windows was observable the name of Johnson; whilst the costumier exhibited that of Thompson.

Near the latter, and under the same roof, opened the doors of two very different offices. The first was supposed to be that of a ship broker, and its next door neighbour, a bill discounter and money changer. The windows of these offices were darkened by thick blinds, which, added to the ab-sence of any sign or designation, gave them a gloomy and mysterious appearance. Nevertheless it was naturally presumed that nothing extraordinary or unusual occurred therein, since it was known that during the day people were observed to enter and transact business as elsewhere.

Next to the brokers, another door opened into the shop of a dealer in trinkets and curiosities. This was equally sombre, nameless, and mysterious, as far as outward appearances went.

Finally, at the back of this extensive building, where it occupied the entire side of a narrow, gloomy, but otherwise respectable square or court, opened ten or twelve iron-barred windows, the lower portion of whose small panes were covered with whitening as a security against the prying regards of the curious.

In the centre of this building was the entrance to the offices of Armstrong and Co.; and though it was well known that they occupied the whole of that extensive range o' premises, yet no one could tell how, or with what they were filled. That was a mystery which incessantly occupied the speculative researches of the smaller shopkeepers in Mint lane, as well as the larger houses of the neighbourhood. Some presumed that Armstrong and Co. dealt in foreign merchandise; but that idea appeared extremely vague and unsatisfactory.

Men were incessantly observed to arrive with packages of every size, form, and colour; carts and drays frequently stopped at the door—discharged their loading, and went away empty. But nothing was ever seen to *leave* the premises! That, as every one seemed to think, was very singular, very strange, and very mysterious!

In one of the houses on the opposite side of the court lived a certain matron named Brown. She was a worthy creature—" fat, fair, and forty;" extremely kind and obliging, but, withal, very inquisitive. Now Mrs. Brown had an intimate friend whose name was Green, and it is but natural to suppose that these ladies, who seemed inseparable, had doubtless passed many an hour over their tea in wondering what the firm of Armstrong and Co. dealt in.

After discussing the subject for at least three months, without the slightest approach towards a solution of the enigma, accident informed them that two other ladies were similarly occupied, and, in fact, had partially succeeded. It was therefore proposed by Mrs. Brown, and seconded by Mrs. Green, and carried *nemine contradicente*, that the names of Mrs. Blue and Mrs. White be added to the committee, which should proceed with the investigation forthwith.

In other houses, both private and public, the

same speculations occupied the minds of the curious and inquisitive.

There was a meeting on the subject at the Pot and Pipe, where Sam Sole, the snob, took the lead, and acted as chairman. Another select coterie assembled at the Blue Bottle, under the presidency of Tom Travers, the tailor.

The excitement which these discussions caused, momentarily increased as new difficulties arose. Whenever anything occurred that had a tendency to discover the mystery, some one was sure to contradict it, or report circumstances which created greater doubt than ever. But people must know, eventually, it was presumed; and thus they went on with the fruitless inquiry.

Why, it was asked, did no one ever perceive in that extraordinary house, neither desk, clerk, nor master?

Several people had mustered courage enough to penetrate into the entrance office, under various pretexts; but all they discovered was, that the apartment seemed equally divided by a high partition, surmounted by neat trellis-work, behind which blue curtains intercepted all further view.

A porter, in bright red and green livery, who appeared to keep guard in the outward division of the apartment, was the only living being who showed his face in that singular establishment.

Another circumstance connected with this strange business, and which seemed to add to the mystery, was the fact that the jeweller, the clothier, the brokers, and the curiosity-dealer, all came simultaneously and established themselves in Mint Lane, at the precise time that the offices of Armstrong and Co. were opened at the back of the same range of buildings.

People enquired if Armstrong and Co. were the leading partners of these inferior tradesmen; but there was no one in the city who appeared to know, although several shook their heads knowingly, as if they could tell more than was prudent to promulgate.

At length Mrs. Brown, Mrs. Green, Mrs. Blue, and Mrs. White met in committee over an infusion of the best gunpowder; and their "report" was anxiously awaited by the buxom Mrs. Blood, and her neighbours of Bury Street. But they found themselves, notwithstanding the utmost exertion, unable to proceed in the solution of so difficult a problem.

In the meantime, merchandize in sufficient quantity to stock half the warehouses of the city was seen to arrive, but not a particle left. At length, one fine evening, as the indefatigable Mrs. Brown was watching the departure of an empty cart, her attention became riveted to the windows of the first story opposite, which were suddenly opened. An extremely handsome gentleman, magnificently attired, appeared behind the silken curtains, and cast a rapid glance round the court below.

"Who is that handsome person?" murmured Mrs. Brown and at least half-a-dozen fair ones at the same moment.

In an instant afterwards, three expresses were sent off to the ladies Green, Blue, and White, announcing the important fact, and calling a privy council thereon.

It must not be supposed that, during this time, Sam Sole and his friends, as also Tom Travers, with the other tradesmen previously alluded to, were idle or indifferent in the matter. On the contrary, the latter imagined they had secured the best means of ascertaining all that occurred by bribing the watchman of Mint Lane with the payment of ten shillings weekly. Poor simpletons! they little dreamed that the same watchman already received thirty shillings weekly for his various undertakings; and, as if that were not sufficient for this honest pluralist, he actually obtained from the mysterious firm itself more than double those payments for keeping silence!

The party who nightly assembled at the Pot and Pipe, suddenly fancied that they had solved the enigma, for their tout had observed the arrival of twenty or thirty seamen, who evidently came to seek employment, and the house of Armstrong & Co., being manifestly ship-brokers, required their services.

An admirable idea! excellent reasoning!

At the end of a month, however, the very same men were seen to return! which clearly demonstrated that the mystery was not so easily solved. A special meeting was then called, to take into consideration the various reports which had been received by the different members of the body.

It was first announced that Jem Jones had been told by Tom Tape, that Ben Brace heard his friend Simon Simple saw six long cases, of a strange and suspicious shape, taken into the warehouse of Armstrong & Co.; and it was accordingly determined that the said Simon Simple should be called in and examined thereon. This was done, when Mr. Simple reiterated his former declarations, and added the astounding information that at the end of one case, which was broken, he beheld the feet of a full grown corpse!

Then a member declared that he had observed several well-known mendicants enter the office in the dead of the night, and were seen no more!

It was further added, that a report was in circulation of a celebrated brigand of the night, and notorious swindler, having arrived there late one evening, when he found his pursuers somewhat too close upon his track, and what had since become of him no one knew.

Various other statements, equally extraordinary and astounding, were received by the little coterie at the Pot and Pipe. All agreed in one thing, namely, that the establishment of Armstrong & Co., large as it was, could not possibly hold a twentieth part of what it received. And yet no one ever saw a single thing sent away from that mysterious house. The excitement became enormous.

At the expiration of another month, those seafaring men, whom we have previously described, arrived in a considerable body. Again, at the end of the following month, they were observed to return. It was impossible, therefore, that they could be sailors.

But what were they then?

That was a question which, like all others connected with the house of Armstrong & Co., no one could answer satisfactorily. People attributed to them various occupations; and some went so far as to hint at unheard of things—of dark associations and secret conspiracies—of criminal transactions, and contraband trafficking!

Be that as it may, the day after the ball at Littlemore house was that appointed for the supposed sailors to pay another visit to the house of Armstrong & Co. About eleven o'clock in the morning, they were seen to arrive in small detachments, and enter the waiting room, or portion of the office in front of the trellised partition already described.

The porter in glaring livery seemed to recognise each of them, for he nodded familiarly and allowed them to enter.

There were fifty-five in number. When the last man had passed the threshold, the porter closed, double-bolted the door, and retired.

The fifty-five new comers were nearly all robust, jovial, and determined-looking fellows. The features of many bore those traces of habitual debauchery which uninterrupted indulgence invariably leaves; some of them preserved on their uncouth cheeks the scars and wounds of many a midnight encounter; others exhibited the traces of rude health and good living which the smoky air of London can by no means secure. The latter did not appear to have long revelled in the dust of town, but there was that sinister cast of expression in the physiognomy of each, that would rather have led one to have avoided them on a dark night, while passing through some secluded lane or deserted road in the open country; for they really possessed the leading characteristics of daring and intrepid outlaws. Except in costume, the jovial

and bold companions of the renowned Robin Hood must have been very much like them in appearance.

Amongst them were two or three young men, who had scarcely passed their "teens," that seemed to add variety to the band.

A great portion of these men have already passed under our notice, and the reader might have recognised in this distinguished assembly several of our nocturnal watermen and mendicants of the street.

There might be seen the amiable Black Bob, who, by the light of day, we must say had all the appearance of a burker; the fat Bill Bull, Boxer, and Stringer, who, on the memorable aquatic excursion, were commanded by the jovial Captain Cable; Groper, the barker, and little Weasel, the mewer—together with several others, with whose names it is not essential we should trouble the reader. All were there except the renowned Captain Cable.

From time to time, each of the jovial fellows assembled in the waiting division of the office cast his eyes anxiously towards a small aperture in the trellis-work before described, and over which was written the magic word "CASH!" It was, therefore, quite evident that those men were sufficiently well informed to be able to comprehend a word so interesting to all.

The majority were seated on forms disposed round the sides of the room, whilst some were standing in little groups whispering brief sentences, or making short inquiries of one another. There was one, however, who stood alone in a recess, and gazing at the panes, whose transparency was concealed under a thick coat of whiting.

At first sight, one would have supposed that he was endeavouring to see through that dark blind; but, on considering him more minutely, it must have been perceived that a subject of more material importance occupied his thoughts. He was engaged in computing the amount of money which he had acquired in various ways during the last few days. That man was no other than Black Bob, the would-be assassin of St. Mary's Church.

The fifty-four companions of Black Bob had for some time been anxiously waiting in the office of Armstrong and Co., when a voice called out from behind the blue curtains—

"Are you all there?"

"Yes, Mr. Matthews," replied the powerful Billy Bull, who appeared to exercise considerable influence over the rest of his companions.

"Yes, we be all here," repeated little Weasel.

Presently a movement was heard behind the curtains, and the grating sound of a key turning in a strong lock brought a smile to the countenances of those who heard it.

"How stupid I am," said the invisible Mr. Matthews; "I have forgotten to get my bank notes changed. Here, Roger!"

As no one appeared to answer the summons, he violently rang a bell. Roger, the porter in glaring livery, immediately entered through an inner door into the small apartment where Mr. Matthews was stationed. The latter then handed to Roger a small roll of bank notes.

"Get these changed for gold as quickly as possible," said he.

"Did ye hear that, my lads?" said Billy Bull in an under tone.

"Oh, yes, Billy, my boy (replied Fat Dick); they be gone to fetch our ribbon."

"Ay, the tin, lads—the tin!" added Weasel.

"Hold yer tongue, ye little viper (continued Dick); Billy knows vot's vot."

"Ay (grumbled Weasel), an' ve knows too."

After a moment's silence, Bill Bull slowly turned round again, and stealthily mounted the bench, in order to look over the curtains.

"Vot the devil be'st thee doin' on?" demanded Boxer in an under tone.

"Ay, Billy, vot's up there?" added the sharp voice of little Weasel.

Billy slowly descended from the bench, stepped into the midst of his companions, and placed his finger to his lips.

"Hush!" he whispered.

"Hush! hush!" imitated Weasel, with a gesture by way of suggesting the propriety of keeping silence.

Stringer pulled the little fellow's ear till it turned blue.

"I'll strangle thee some day, thou miserable son of a prig," murmured he.

Weasel mewed plaintively. Bill Bull assembled his select friends around him.

"There (said he in an under tone, and pointing

at the same time towards the curtains), behind Mr. Matthews—about two yards from his stool—is a great iron chest wide open."

"Vell?"

"In that chest there is——"

"Tin," "Ribbon," "Gold!" interrupted several voices at once.

"No."

"So much the vorse."

"No gold?" "No tin?" "No ribbon?" cried the group.

"In the ruffian's name, be quiet, vill ye?" murmured Bill Bull. "The fust as speaks so loud agin I'll knock into the middle of next veek."

On hearing this threat, Weasel prudently retired into the rear of the group.

"No gold?" repeated Stringer with a frown;—"then vot the devil's in it?"

"It's full of bank notes," whispered Billy.

Every eye became instantly lighted up, and the under-current of a dull murmur arose from the group that surrounded Bill Bull.

"In that 'ere box there's tin enough to make a fortin for every one on us!"

The murmurs increased tenfold as these words were pronounced. An eager avidity seemed to creep over every countenance, and each eye was immediately directed towards the curtain.

"Steady, my lads," whispered Bull; "be quiet a bit."

"Patience men, have a little patience," said Mr. Matthews in a loud tone.

The latter, who mistook these murmurs for uneasiness, was seated at his desk, tranquilly perusing the close columns of a newspaper.

It is impossible we can give our readers any idea of his features, for they appeared almost entirely covered. His neck and chin were enveloped in the ample folds of an enormous comforter; a mask concealed the upper portion of his face; and, finally, a large pair of green spectacles added singularity to the whole.

"Fortin?" murmured little Weasel; "it would be capital to get a fortin easy."

"So I thinks," added Groper.

"My lads," said a voice which had not yet been heard amongst them; "I'd settle the bisniss more quieter, if I vos you."

"Black Bob!" exclaimed one and all, "vhere the devil did you come from? ve didn't see ye afore."

Bob had quietly left the position which he previously occupied near the window, to join the group that surrounded Bill Bull. Every one turned towards the amiable personage who had thus suddenly appeared amongst them. Black Bob made a motion

with his hand to secure silence, winked an eye, and said in an under tone,—

"I never makes more noise than is vanted, my lads; I've been here as long as any of ye, but ye didn't know it, cos I keeps quiet! Yes, I has been lookin' arter you all the mornin', by the guvner's desire; howsumever, if I'd known ye wor goin' on in this vay—"

"Stop yer gans (lips), muster Soapy (hypocrite)," interrupted Bill Bull; "you'll be the fust to jine us, I knows. I tell ye there's piles of bank notes behind there! and it ain't right they should lie still and rot, is it?"

"No, it ain't, by no means," rejoined Bob in a morose voice; "it's confounded temptin' I must say; and if one could go to work quietly—I—the captain won't be here, that's a good job!"

"No, Captain Cable ain't likely to be here," said Weasel.

"It's devilish tempting!" repeated Bob in a thoughtful tone.

After a moment's reflection he glided towards the partition, which he cautiously shook.

"Patience men," exclaimed Mr. Matthews, who was still reading the newspaper.

"It's strong," muttered Bob in a whisper.

"Strong!" repeated Bull with indifference; "hark ye, lads, be ye men enough to follow me?"

"Yes, I'll swing if ve ain't," replied little Weasel.

"Vot's to be done?" inquired several of the group.

Bull did not waste time in replying to those questions, but at once rushed forward with impetuous force, thrusting the well-nailed heel of his massive shoe against the central panel of the partitioning which supported the trellis-work. The curtains were very much shaken by the blow, but nothing fell or was displaced.

"What is that?" said Mr. Matthews in an angry voice.

Bull was about to renew the attack, but Black Bob stopped him.

"You make a great deal too much noise," said he in a deprecating tone; "ye should alvays manage in sich a vay that only one blow would do the bisniss."

Without taking any spring, or apparently making any effort, he struck the lock so violently with his iron heel, that it fell down with a tremendous crash. In accomplishing this feat, he was slightly driven on one side, which enabled the group in front to rush into the private office of Mr. Matthews.

"I only struck it once," he murmured with satisfaction, "but that was enough."

While our fifty-five besiegers were storming the

private apartment, Mr. Matthews, (warned by the report of the first attack led by Bill Bull), was endeavouring to put himself in a state of defence. His first object was to secure the cash box, for which purpose, after rapidly closing it, he hastily rolled his desk between the door and the chest; but in his hurry and confusion, a portion of his coat became entangled with the handles of the desk, and rendered all his efforts fruitless.

"Don't trouble yerself to move that desk, Mr. Matthews," observed Bill Bull; "it ain't vorth vile, seein as how we can do it ourselves."

Mr. Matthews, however, did not appear to think it any trouble, but, on the contrary, exerted himself still more vigorously.

"It's too late to put yerself in our vay, I tell ye," resumed Bill Bull; "and so you'd better take care. Now if ye'll be civil and quiet, ve'll give ye one half on it—that's fair."

"No, no, no," cried the band, "it's a great deal too much."

"I say agin, one half," repeated Bill Bull peremptorily.

"Listen!" exclaimed Mr. Matthews, whose neckerchief had fallen from his chin in the scuffle, and exposed to view the lower portion of his face, which was pale as death.

"Before touching that box," said he, in a firm voice, "you shall walk over my dead body to the spot where it stands."

"Oh, that is easily done," replied Bill Bull, with brutal indifference.

An immoderate burst of laughter from the group followed the utterance of those words.

"Ay, ay, that could easily be done," repeated little Weasel; "I'll swing if it couldn't."

Black Bob pushed his repulsive head, replete with cunning, behind the door-way, and directed his artful glances towards the extremity of the office.

"It looks vell," he murmured, "but I've seen sich jokes as this turn on them as begins 'em, afore now."

The interior of the private office formed nearly one half of the apartment, and was furnished as such places usually are; on the right opened a door which communicated with the immense warehouse that belonged to the firm of Armstrong & Co. To the left was a large winding staircase, leading to the apartments on the first floor.

In their eagerness for plunder, the assailants had not taken the trouble to notice all that—they had other matters to attend to of more consequence at that moment. Whilst Bull, Stringer, and others were turning the desk which Mr. Matthews had thrown down as a rampart before the cash-box, another of the band, more agile or eager than the rest, leaped upon a table that stood near the chest, and with an exultation quite characteristic, exclaimed,—

"The fust for me!"

"Bravo, Groper!" shouted the throng.

Mr. Matthews recoiled a step or two, and regarded the intruder with an air of determined resolution.

"Yes, thou shalt have the first," he repeated ironically; at the same moment plunging one hand in each of his capacious pockets, from whence he withdrew a pair of double-barrelled pistols.

With a slight curl of the upper lip, from which all colour had completely disappeared, he raised one of the pistols, and directed a steady aim at the approaching figure. Groper staggered backwards, and his brains flew over the nearest assailants, which made them recoil at the terrible check they had thus received.

"Ah, that's it, is it?" observed Black Bob, retreating as far as the entrance door.

The other besiegers, however, did not follow his example; on the contrary, Bill Bull, and Dick, rushed forward, and threw down Mr. Matthews while in the act of aiming a second pistol at his assailants. Bull then sought for his knife, with the view to cut the throat of his prostrate foe.

Just at that moment, however, something strange and extraordinary was taking place. All the assailants, with the exception of Bill Bull and Dick, suddenly becoming seized with a panic, precipitately followed the example of Black Bob, and hurriedly retired behind the trellised partition; leaving the bleeding corpse of Groper extended on the table. Each one endeavoured to conceal himself in the best way he could, and with the downcast look of children, when corrected by a severe master, remained silent and motionless.

But what caused this unusual terror in the minds of beings apparently so abandoned and obdurate? Let us see.

At the report of the pistol, which was scarcely heard at all in the street, but which must have loudly resounded through the more immediate apartments of the house, an august-looking personage, with a black mask, showed himself at the top of the winding staircase, and was gazing on the scene below. Then, without uttering a single word, he slowly descended the steps till he came within five or six of the bottom. All the men had seen him with the exception of Bill and Dick, both of whom, as we have seen, were seriously occupied at the time.

After gazing around him for a few moments, the masked man unconcernedly turned towards the cashier.

"What was all that noise about, Mr. Matthews?" he coldly inquired; "you know that I require repose; pray, therefore, see that silence be restored."

"The guv'ner!" feebly articulated Bull, in a tone of the utmost alarm.

Dick immediately assumed a suppliant attitude.

"Pardon! pardon! my lord duke!" he tremulously ejaculated, quivering with fear.

"They be sorely pinched!" murmured Black Bob in the obscurity of his favourite corner. "I al'ys thought that them stairs led somewhere!"

The masked slowly returned by the way that he came; whilst Bill and Dick went with a pitiful air and rejoined their companions.

Mr. Matthews had already raised himself, put his desk in order, and was preparing to resume his occupation.

"I must get rid of that lumber," said he with a glance at the body of Groper.

"Yes, Mr. Matthews," responded Bill Bull, respectfully; "ve must take it away for ye."

Mr. Matthews once more opened the newspaper, and recommenced reading as if nothing unusual had occurred to interrupt him.

—o—

CHAPTER X.

HERE AND THERE.

The fifty-four individuals, who, a few minutes previously, had besieged the office of Armstrong & Co., remained a short time under the effects of that powerful impression which the apparition that had so suddenly put an end to the disturbance created. The impression was, undoubtedly, most profound, for they had not ventured to articulate another word. The corpulent Dick tried to hide himself behind the less stout Bull, who, in his turn, endeavoured to conceal his person behind little Weasel. No one could very well shelter himself behind Black Bob, since that lovely personage had artfully encrusted himself, as it were, in the wall itself.

Out of doors, some of the neighbours fancied they had heard a noise like the report of a pistol; a most sagacious idea, under the circumstances, it must be admitted. Mrs. Green accordingly repaired to Mrs. Brown, whom she conducted to Mrs. Blue, who joined them in a visit to Mrs. White; at the house of the latter, Mrs. Moore took Mrs. Munn to witness that the nameless building was inhabited by the devil himself, under the assumed name of Armstrong & Co. Mrs. Tongue and Mrs. Magg gave it as their opinion that the idea was by no means improbable.

These ladies conversed much upon that topic, till at length they had settled the matter satisfac-

torily to themselves, and every doubt was drowned in copious libations of the best gunpowder.

After the lapse of some minutes, Weasel, who was by no means pleased with the position he occupied, made a movement to improve it; Dick immediately recovered himself; and Bill Bull coughed cautiously. Thus the ice was broken, and each felt somewhat relieved.

"Poor Groper!" exclaimed Bill Bull.

"Poor Groper!" repeated Stringer, unaffectedly.

"Poor Groper!" added Weasel, in a lamentable tone; "he barked so well!"

This little rascal was a singular and precocious son of a mendicant. He appeared to be about seventeen years of age at most, but his pale yellow face was somewhat wrinkled, and resembled that of an old man. His features had a double expression; sometimes they were brightened by a smile of maliciousness truly diabolical; and then they would assume an appearance of complete brutality. Slightly deformed, he was scarcely equal in his proportions to a child twelve years of age. His frail limbs, devoid of muscular power, by no means denoted a state of puberty. Like every child, whether good or bad, he seemed anxious to raise himself to the importance of a man, and had, consequently, descended a great number of steps down the ladder of evil, in order to have some pretension to consideration amongst those by whom he was surrounded.

"Why didn't Mr. Matthews tell us at once that his honour was up above?" growled Boxer.

"Ye might easily ha' known that," said Black Bob, in an under tone, "if there hadn't been so much noise. As to my lord, he'd be deuced clever as could tell afore hand vhere his honour vould be found."

"You know him better nor any on us, Bob," interrupted Bull with an eager curiosity.

"Me? not I indeed! I only troubles myself about my own affairs; as to poor Groper, why Mr. Matthews did quite right, an' that's settled."

"Poor Groper!" again repeated several of the more humane members of the group. And little Weasel lamentably added,—

"Poor feller, he vont bark agin!"

Black Bob now left his corner and approached the body, which he examined with the air of a connoisseur.

"He vos a jolly feller," observed Bob, critically. "He'll make a good 'un for the doctors; and one could easily get three megs for him, I'm thinking. Who'll help me to carry him away?"

"Nobody shall touch him," exclaimed Bull; "he belongs to me now."

"How so?" inquired Bob, angrily.

"Because," replied Bill, affecting to wipe away a tear, " Groper was my pal—my best friend; and I ought at least to have the benefit of all as is left on him."

This irresistible argument was admitted by the whole band, and the body of Groper immediately delivered over to Bull, his best friend; in order that the said Bill should dispose of it to the best advantage.

Black Bob left the body with a grin of disappointment, muttering as he did so,—

"I'll be revenged on ye for this, my boy, afore long, depend on it."

At that moment, Wilson, the domestic in showy livery, entered the office, unconscious of the misfortune which his delay had occasioned. He, however, did not manifest the slightest surprise on perceiving the body of Groper; from which it must be presumed that such scenes were familiar to his eye; or that most mysterious things frequently took place in the office of Armstrong & Co.

He handed over to Mr. Matthews two heavy bags, the contents of which proved to be gold, and were immediately placed upon his desk.

Mr. Matthews then counted out fifty-five sums of five guineas each; after which he took from one of his drawers a list on which was written fifty-five names, and began to call out. Every time he pronounced a name, one man presented himself before the cashier and received five guineas, and retired.

At the name of Groper, Bill Bull and Black Bob simultaneously presented themselves.

"I vas his best friend," observed Bull, with marked emphasis.

"You have had his body," persisted Bob, who stretched out his hand for the purpose of seizing the gold.

The robust Bull clenched his enormous fist.

"If thee touchest it," said he, "I'll knock ye down!"

Bob put his hand underneath his coat, and felt the blade of an enormous knife, which never went out of his possession; at the same time his eyes appeared to dilate, and shoot forth vivid flashes. Bull became quite pale, and already fancied that he felt the cold steel pierce his heart. Black Bob thought better of it, however, and regained his corner with a very peaceable step. The fact is he had just seen Mr. Matthews withdraw the five guineas and place them in his drawer; consequently there was nothing left to quarrel about. Master Bull had also noticed this at the same moment, and his first idea was to rush on Mr. Matthews with the view to secure it to himself; but on second consideration he altered his mind.

"If it vosn't for his honour, who is the devil himself, or some'ot vorse," he muttered between his set teeth, and with difficulty repressing his increasing anger, "I'd knock yer green specs into yer brains, if ye have any, old feller."

Mr. Matthews probably heard that amiable remark, for a brief smile of satisfaction, mingled with contempt, played upon his lip; he did not, however, appear to notice it.

The last heap of gold was taken from the aperture in the partition at the moment the final name was called out by the cashier.

"Now," observed Mr. Matthews, n a cold and morose tone, pointing at the same time to the body of Groper; "rid me of the remains of that confounded brigand, and take care ye are all wiser in future. *Here* I don't permit any one to intrude, except his lordship; *there*, however," continued the cashier, pointing to the waiting division of the office, "you may do what you please. *Here* and *there* are two places, as you will know to your cost the next time you attempt to repeat the tricks of this morning."

"Ve mun have a sack and some straw, if ye please, Mr. Matthews," observed Bill Bull, meekly, as he cast a rapid and satisfied glance over the corpse.

The cashier directed Wilson to fetch what was required, and in a few moments the servant in glaring livery returned therewith. In the twinkling of an eye, the corpse was packed up like a bale of bacon, and with as much indifference. It was then placed on the powerful shoulders of Bill Bull, who at once departed, accompanied by all his companions, with the exception of Black Bob.

"What are you doing there?" said Mr. Matthews to the latter, who had again resumed his calculating attitude.

"I'm vaitin' for his honor," replied Bob; "the Duke vill be glad to see me."

"The Duke!" exclaimed Mr. Matthews with surprise. "You are mad, man!"

Bob threw a rapid glance all round the room.

"Not quite, sir (said he); the Duke——"

"I would strongly advise you not to repeat that name again, my friend—at least, unless you have a desire to follow Master Groper out of the world."

"Vell, vell," resumed Bob meekly, "I thought as how it vould be all right 'twixt you and me, sir. Howsomdever, his lordship does vont to see me."

"What can his lordship want with thee?"

"I don't know, Mr. Matthews; p'raps it's to give me summut for my family—p'raps somethin' else; all I can tell is, he 'xpects me."

"Wilson," cried Mr. Matthews, "go and ask his lordship if he wishes to receive this fellow."

"No," interrupted Bob abruptly; "I don't like ceremonies at all. S'pose ye goes and asks his honor if he vants to speak to Black Bob."

In a few moments the domestic returned and beckoned to Black Bob, who immediately ascended the spiral staircase which led to the first suite of apartments. He traversed the hall, or ante-room, preceded by Wilson, and waited in an apartment superbly furnished, while being announced. Although scarcely five seconds had elapsed before the domestic reappeared to conduct him to his master, yet an experienced thief like Black Bob, found that amply sufficient to convey into the vast depths of his capacious pockets about half a dozen articles of value.

"This will do for Steady," thought he, on appropriating to himself a magnificent handkerchief.

The apartment into which he had entered was nearly opposite that occupied by Mrs. Brown, who had for her next door neighbours Dr. Dawson, his mother, and beautiful cousins. Upon the removal of the arras, our handsome dreamer of St. Mary's church was observed partly reclining on a velvet couch, and smoking an oriental pipe with a long amber tube. He seemed pale and rakish, and his appearance indicated that satiated indolence which is the invariable result of a whole night's dissipation. Before him stood a little negro, who held wide open a large book, on the pages of which the gentleman from time to time cast his distracted look.

On the seat of an arm-chair near his side were placed a black mask, a rapier, and a four-barrelled pistol. We have already seen the mask, and it is probable that, had the besiegers made further resistance, we should also have heard several reports from the pistol as his lordship descended the spiral stair-case.

At the moment when Bob's footsteps were heard in the adjoining apartment, Mr. Armstrong instinctively took up his mask, and, by a rapid movement, fixed it over his face. No sooner, however, did Bob make his appearance, than the mask was again taken off and replaced by his side.

Bob advanced slowly, saluting right and left, till his nose almost touched the magnificent carpet which covered the floor. Mr. Armstrong made a sign with his head, which sent the little negro away from his presence.

"What do you want with me, Bob, my beauty?"

The latter called to his repulsive features a crafty smile, and replied,

"I have come, yer honor, about that little bisniss ye knows on."

Bob involuntarily winked his eye on pronouncing the last word.

"I know nothing of it," observed Mr. Armstrong, in a languid tone. "Come, explain yourself more clearly, and be brief, too."

"I vill, then, yer honor: but has ye already forgot the little mendicant of St. Mary's Church? Ah!" continued Bob, in a tone of admiration, "*I* ain't forgot how easy she gets ten pun' notes of the gentry!"

Mr. Armstrong did not appear to recollect, at least his thoughts were evidently bent on other matters; but those few words were sufficient to recall to his memory the fascinating scenes of the church. The sensations which he had experienced in that sacred edifice were at once sweet and powerful! nevertheless, for the moment they appeared lost in oblivion, for he slowly drew his hands over his eyes as if to collect those fugitive images.

"Yes," said he, after a few moments' silence; "she is an enchanting creature, truly. What exquisite sweetness shone in her features! what simplicity in her looks, and modesty in her melodious voice!"

"Yes! yer honour," added Bob, who could not forget that she alone was able to collect ten-pound notes; "for a mendicant, she is a reg'lar angel!"

Mr. Armstrong dropped his hand, and cast a scrutinizing glance on the smiling countenance of Black Bob.

"I gave thee an order," he observed; "did I not?"

"Yes, yer honour; exactly. And that's the reason I'm come to see yer honour."

"Well, what was the result?"

"Vhy, it's jist this, yer honour: I follered the young lady—I means the ladies, for there vas two on 'em—with a young man."

"A young gentleman?"

"Yes, yer honour. And, talkin' of that, I must tell ye that he asked werry perticler who you vos!"

"Who asked you that?"

"The young genl'man, yer honour. And vot's more, he gives me two bright megs—guineas, I means, yer honour—for my trouble."

It must be admitted that master Bob was wrong in mentioning double the amount he had received from Dr. Dawson; but then we must recollect that, in consequence of the peculiar formation of his eyes, he generally saw twice as much as other people, especially when it suited his purpose; and this to some extent, perhaps, explains the reason for his present assertion.

"And what did you tell him?" inquired Mr. Armstrong.

"Nothin' at all, yer honour—not a single vord! And, sure enough, I vos werry vell paid for it—two bright m— guineas!"

"Well! and where does the young girl reside?— you found that out, of course?"

"Ah! yer honour vont have far to go; ye vont have to take a carrige vhen ye vishes to pay her a wisit! I vos jist sayin' to myself, ses I—"

"Where does she reside?" interrupted Mr. Armstrong, impatiently.

As the dark cloud of anger appeared to be gathering on the handsome features of Mr. Armstrong, Black Bob deemed it necessary to repress his obsequious smile, which was instantly replaced by an air of serious diffidence.

"Close by," replied the latter; "in short, it's right oppersite ye, on the other side of the square!"

The gentleman, whom for the present we shall still call Armstrong, turned quickly round and followed the gesture of Bob, which indicated the window of the second-floor on the opposite side of the court. His movement was so rapid that the exquisite figure of a young girl, which was partially visible behind the curtains, had not sufficient time for concealment. Mr. Armstrong directed towards her a glance, which, one might safely say, contained in it three or four declarations of love at least. The moment the young girl discovered that she was recognised, she became scarlet with blushing; her eyes closed, and the curtain fell.

"It is she!" exclaimed Mr. Armstrong enthusiastically. "I could not distinguish her hair; but I am convinced it is she! How do you know that she lives on that floor?"

"I'll tell yer honour werry soon," replied Bob. "In the fust place, seein' as how I couldn't go and knock at people's doors, vhen one considers that my livery aint by no means kalkerlated to command respect, it seemed to me as how I must contrive some artful dodge to get the perticklers yer honour vanted. Howsomever, when the two young ladies and the genleman entered that house there, I stops below here, jist oppersite. Vhile I vas vaitin to see their movements, I jist looks up at the vinders, and seed every one on 'em lighted up 'xcept them on the second floor, vhere, in one minnit, light appeared like t'others—jist at the momint that they could have got into the room and stirred up the fire."

Mr. Armstrong doubtless considered that explanation satisfactory, for he made a sign with his head by way of approbation.

"That will do," said he. "Desire Mr. Matthews to pay you for your trouble."

"I'd a good deal rather yer honour vould obleege me vith the money yerself, if it be pleasing to yer honour," observed Bob, with humility.

"Why?"

"It's hard to get a livin' anyhow, and—"

"And what?" inquired Mr. Armstrong, finding that Bob hesitated about his reply.

"Mr. Matthews will say that he has already paid me, yer honour."

Mr. Armstrong thereupon threw down two guineas, and dismissed him with a gesture. Bob kissed the pieces of gold with reverence, like a true mendicant as he was.

"God bless yer honour!" he exclaimed, in the habitual tone of his tribe. And, on retiring, he added, "Forty-two bob only! It's d—n—n bad, vhen he gives ten-pun' notes to lady mendicants, 'cause they don't vant it, and is pretty! That ain't right, by no means. It strikes me as how that young man vould be more free vith his tin!—I've a confounded good mind to try!"

Mr. Armstrong still remained on his velvet couch, and continued to gaze at the window opposite. He recalled to mind the enchanting scene at St. Mary's Church, and endeavoured to rebuild in imagination one of those aerial palaces in which he had so sweetly reposed that evening. Occasionally, thoughts of a less agreeable nature would intrude themselves upon him, but he shook them off, and jealously enjoyed the delicious extacy of his dreamy repose.

He was so much absorbed in the laborious enjoyment of a voluntary dreamer, that he did not perceive the curtains of the opposite window again raised, and the beautiful face of Caroline Jones show itself for the second time. That young girl, however, directed towards him one of those earnest and piercing glances which Dr. Dawson, her cousin, had deemed so strange on the Sunday evening in St. Mary's Church. Her eye rested ardently and sorrowfully on the handsome countenance of Mr. Armstrong, and she seemed unable to withdraw it. She was much paler than on the Sunday evening alluded to. There were traces of tears underneath her eyelids, and her cheeks bore evidence of having passed many sleepless nights.

Nevertheless, as she continued to regard the handsome sleeper opposite, her whole physiognomy gradually became illumined by a serene smile; her sadness gave place to melancholy, which transformed itself into feeble and solemn happiness. Thus she appeared more beautiful than ever. Her heart beat with joy; her lips became pale, and tremulously murmured unconnected sentences.

Caroline loved the handsome dreamer, passionately; she regarded him with that profound, exalted, and intoxicating love, which solitude and study in such cases engender.

Caroline and her younger sister had passed their infancy in the midst of one of the most beautiful landscapes, with which the greater part of Wales so luxuriantly abounds. At that age when every young girl more particularly requires the care and attentions of a mother, Caroline and Jane had the misfortune to lose theirs. Mr. Jones kept them under his own care, and watched over them very affectionately for three or four years. Then, suddenly—while his children were still very young, though old enough to notice the circumstance—Mr. Jones's conduct became completely changed, and enveloped in a strange mystery. Unknown persons were received at his mansion, and he had frequently long conferences with them. He also undertook secret journeys, with the object of which none of his old friends were made acquainted.

It was about this time that he entreated his sister, Mrs. Dawson, whom family affairs retained in London, to take charge of his two daughters.

When musing on that event, Caroline could not but think that her father had seemed anxious to relieve himself of their infantine superintendence, and that he had mysterious reasons for being thus left alone.

At the time that proposition was made to Mrs. Dawson, the latter had not long been a widow, and had scarcely recovered from the terrible affliction which suddenly overwhelmed her. Her husband had been assassinated !

Mrs. Dawson received her nieces with an affable cordiality. As her grief, at first most poignant, gradually abated, she more fully appreciated the charming dispositions of her nieces. It is true that the young girls did not much resemble each other in every respect, but then they were both equally amiable and good, and Mrs. Dawson soon felt for them the tenderness of a mother.

Every time that Mr. Jones came to London— and it must be admitted that his visits were not frequent—the worthy old lady trembled lest he should take his daughters back with him. She need not have been apprehensive on that point, however; Mr. Jones had not the slightest idea of doing so. The short time he remained, was invariably passed in rapid excursions about town, and which he always explained by that simple word "business!" an admirable expression for the purpose, and especially invented to evade every attempt at curiosity. At each new visit, Caroline and Jane remarked, with increasing alarm, the sad change which was taking place in their parent, who seemed to be rapidly becoming a premature old man. He was scarcely fifty, and yet his pale forehead no longer preserved a single particle of its former intelligence. Grief, the more intense because it was concealed, seemed to carry desolation to his once vigorous frame. His affectionate daughters would gladly have poured consolation over that hidden

sorrow, whose effects were so palpably apparent, had they known its source; but Mr. Jones did not like to be questioned thereon. Caroline and Jane, thus abruptly repulsed, no longer persevered in their affectionate solicitude for the welfare of their parent, but contented themselves with silently lamenting his altered state.

Dr. Dawson, like his mother, as we have already shown, was very much attached to his cousins. The diabolical assassination of his father, of which terrible event accident made him a witness, had at first severely shaken his faculties. But at the period when that occurred he was very young, and as he grew, time at length brought back his infantile intelligence. Still, however, the recollection of his dying father, and that of the assassin, were firmly engraven in traces of blood on his memory. The murderer, whom he saw for a moment only as the mask which he wore fell from his face, (of which he had simply a partial glance,) was not so indelibly impressed on his recollection; nevertheless, one circumstance, clear and precise, remained fixed in the depth of his remembrance. He recollected seeing before him a tall, vigorous, and supple man, who, (at the moment when the mask fell and for an instant discovered his features,) struck the fatal blow. In that diabolical effort, the assassin's dark eyes frowned, and graphically portrayed on his flushed forehead the tremulous line of a long scar. And Dr. Dawson believed he again perceived the same mark on the handsome features of the dreaming cavalier in St. Mary's church !

Dr. Dawson was a Welshman, although brought up in London—that grand centre of the material world, and which, in fact, is a world in itself. He was educated at Oxford, where he had passed some of the most agreeable portion of his youth. During his sojourn at the university, he had formed a most intimate acquaintance with a fellow-student—a friendship which became sincere and lasting. Dawson and his friend were much attached to each other; the more so, perhaps, from the circumstance of their being so very different, both in position and appearance. One was the descendant of a humble citizen, whilst the other belonged to the highest nobility. The handsome son of a proud, romantic, and luxurious nobleman, contrasted materially with the more business-like physician, whose character was not wanting in firmness or true nobility. The friend of Dr. Dawson was the Honourable Henry Vernon.

The young physician had become somewhat sad since the scene in St. Mary's church, of which we have already spoken. That, indeed, was an eventful day in the life of Dr. Dawson. He had then suddenly made a positive choice between his two

cousins, whom, hitherto, he had loved with equal affection. His passion, which, from various causes, had remained in a latent state, now burst forth with uncontrollable violence. His mode of life became changed, and he suffered that languor which first-love instils into the hearts of those least suspected of sensibility.

Dr. Dawson had been invited to the ball at Littlemore House. Now a grand ball is an attraction perfectly irresistible for a young man of Dr. Dawson's age; especially when it introduces him to a new and glittering world. And such was the case with our young physician. Born in the vicinity of Holywell House, where Lord Littlemore possessed several magnificent estates, he by that means gained patronage and esteem which had formerly been bestowed on his father. Lord Littlemore, to whom he had a short time previously been introduced, received him as the son of a revered friend, and had voluntarily classed himself amongst

the future patrons of the young physician. Dr. Dawson consequently received a letter of invitation to the ball, which had much occupied his thoughts during the eight long days that preceded it. Nevertheless, when the hour arrived, instead of preparing his toilet, the young physician sat musing ill-humouredly in an arm-chair, and apparently contemplating the fantastic forms of the embers in his extinct fire.

Shortly after the clock had struck ten, Mrs. Dawson softly rapped at his door.

"Well, David, my dear," said she, "are you dressing?"

"I would have given six months of my life for each of those bewitching glances which she directed towards the pillar," muttered Dr. Dawson, with enthusiasm.

That response must give an admirable idea of the young physician's thoughts at the moment. In fact his whole soul seemed absorbed in the contemplation of his beautiful cousin, and the detestable stranger of St. Mary's church, who was at once so handsome, rich, and powerful!

"Do you not think of going to the ball?" again inquired the old lady.

"What would be the utility of it?" observed Dr. Dawson; "what should I do amongst those proud nobles who would either laugh at or treat me with cold disdain? I begin to detest the aristocracy, mother!"

And he added in an under tone—

"I feel confident that such a vain dispenser of ten pound notes is at least a peer!"

"Oh, David," rejoined Mrs. Dawson, in a reproachful tone, "you forget that your poor father enjoyed the esteem of every nobleman in our county. Yes, their esteem and friendship," she continued, with a slight movement of pride.

"Oh! what matters that, mother?" interrupted the physician with impatience.

Mrs. Dawson regarded her son with astonishment.

"How strangely you speak this evening, my dear," she observed; "there must be something the matter I am sure. As to going to the ball, you can do as you please; I have not come to advise you to proceed thither, or to stay at home. Here is a letter for you, which I think comes from an old acquaintance."

"From Harry Vernon!" exclaimed David, anxiously; as a bland smile overspread his countenance.

"I have learned to recognise his hand," observed Mrs. Dawson; "since I found his letters interested you so much."

"He arrives to-day," said David, after hastily perusing the first few lines. "Poor Harry! he, too, will be unhappy."

"He too!" repeated Mrs. Dawson; "are you, then, unhappy, David?"

The latter forced a smile to his countenance, and his amiable mother, thus reassured, left him and retired to bed. Scarcely had she left, when two slight taps were heard at the door, and the sweet voice of a young girl timidly pronounced these words,—

"Thanks, my dear cousin, a thousand thanks!"

Then with a step light as that of the gazelle, she was heard to skip over the steps of the stairs that led to the upper apartments.

It is necessary that we should inform the reader, that during the preceding eight days, the pretty Jane Jones had employed all her eloquence in the hitherto vain endeavour to persuade her cousin from going to the ball at Littlemore House. She, too, had her little jealousies, and, consequently,

entertained a vague idea of the irresistible attractions with which a lady of fashion is surrounded; her instinct vividly depicted the delight which seized a young man on his introduction to those brilliant soirees, where eyes question and reply to each other. It is not surprising, therefore, that she became much alarmed, poor child, for she loved her cousin passionately.

The young physician inclined his head towards the door, and listened eagerly.

"It is the voice of Jane," he murmered in a tone of disappointment after a moment's silence. "Yes, it is the footstep of Jane—poor dear girl! she thinks of me; but Caroline does not come! It doubtless matters but little to her whether I go or not!"

The physician sighed heavily, and pressed his head between his hands like a person who is suffering some profound affliction.

"Ah!" he exclaimed, "how beautiful she looked in the church, and how proud her regard would have rendered me! Oh! how dearly I love her! But I fear my affection will not be reciprocated. But why not? Alas! there is that hateful personage, who appears to monopolize all her thoughts!" added the physician, with a sudden vehemence; then, after a moment's silence, continued, "Who is he? what is he? whence does he come?"

The physician arose and paced the room with irregular steps for a few minutes, after which he reseated himself, and again resumed his thoughtful attitude.

"It strikes me I must have seen him somewhere," he muttered; "indeed, I am pretty certain of it, though I cannot recollect under what circumstances, and yet—it is strange; very mysterious!"

—o—

CHAPTER XI.

THE CENTRE OF MYSTERY.

DR. DAWSON remained in his reflective position for upwards of an hour; at length, after many a vain endeavour to recall to his memory under what circumstances he had previously seen the hateful stranger of St. Mary's church, an idea suddenly entered his mind, which, for a moment, astounded him. His character was one of those to which suspicion has easy access, and which does not readily abandon it when once created. That evening, too, the first thoughts of love, which had just entered his soul, gave another course to his ideas.

"What a fool I am!" he murmured, after a few moment's silence; "she is as pure as the angels, of whose beauty she partakes! But alas! I suffer much in this state of mind. I must see poor Harry Vernon, for he, too, suffers like myself! We will lament together, if we cannot mutually console each other."

Upwards of twelve months had elapsed since Dr. Dawson had seen his friend Harry Vernon; and, moreover, the last time they had met, the interview was short and frivolous. They were then both happy and unmindful of the future; the former had recently heard, by chance, some of those reports concerning Miss Littlemore, which were then in circulation. He was aware, that in circles usually well informed, her approaching marriage with the distinguished De Duro was generally spoken of as almost certain. It was to that circumstance he had made allusion in his conversation with Mrs. Dawson.

The Hon. Henry Vernon and David Dawson were consequently in that position which renders friendship doubly precious, and mutual assistance a necessity. He accordingly awaited the expected meeting with impatience. The delight which he experienced by the thought of seeing Harry again so soon, to some extent subdued the intensity of his sufferings. He did not go to the ball at Littlemore House.

At length he again rose, and though still suffering most acutely, yet his countenance denoted calmness and comparative repose. There is a resource with those hasty characters who do not so greedily feed on the troubles they suffer, nor mournfully give way under the pressure of their grief, but only require a generous sympathy to be consoled.

The young physician, then, had not passed so very indifferently his first night's martyrdom of love; he had no sort of envy for those who attended the ball, because he knew not who might be there; and he promised himself relief from his present suspense and uncertainty by forthwith demanding an explanation from his cousin Caroline Jones. That is what may be called " coming to the point!' Does every lover, under such circumstances, pursue a course so judicious and logical? We fancy not. But then the lover in the present instance was a physician, and the cure of diseases, whether of the mind or body, being a matter of business with him, it is not surprising that he should pass through the first stage of his complaint so extremely well.

At the family breakfast next morning Caroline appeared unusually absent and absorbed by imperitive thoughts. Her cousin of course did not fail to notice it; he was about to address a few words to her on the subject, but checked himself, and resolved to wait for his friend Harry Vernon's advice before he proceeded further in such a delicate affair.

His cousin Jane, on the contrary seemed extremely happy, and overwhelmed him with the warmest expressions of gratitude for acceding to her desire of not attending the ball. Dr. Dawson, however, took no notice thereof, for his thoughts were entirely devoted to her sister. Poor Jane! She firmly believed that her cousin had deprived himself of the pleasure of going to Litlemore House because he loved her too well to act in opposition to her wishes, and the young girl, consequently, could not dissimulate her happiness.

Directly after the breakfast, and whilst the tea-urn was still smoking on the table, Caroline abruptly left the room. We already know whither she then repaired. It was in fact to station herself behind that curtain, which, partly raised, permitted her eye to penetrate into the room of the large mysterious building opposite. Caroline proceeded thither daily, but it was frequently in vain, for the visits of the person she sought were brief and by no means frequent. Nevertheless she did not fail to attend the same spot regularly.

On the day in question, however, she was more fortunate, for she then discovered the object she had sought so assiduously.

We will not attempt to portray the profound and multifarious impressions which rapidly succeeded each other in the mind of the young girl during her mute contemplation whilst standing at the window. It was there she had first seen Mr. Armstrong; and it was to that spot she daily repaired to await his contemplated arrival. At that place she remained for hours: sometimes suffering the worst agonies of suspense; at others, she was extremely happy, and learned to love.

At times she appeared almost unconscious of everything around her, and frequently forgot the actual progress of the hours. When Mr. Armstrong, guided by the gesture of Black Bob, turned his eyes towards her, she felt her heart beat with an emotion at once sweet and poignant. She became somewhat excited; her legs bent under her; and a stream of burning blood flowed through every vein, even to her cheeks, which became scarlet. At that moment her hand released the curtain.

She remained thus for some time, at first ashamed of her proceedings; then affected almost to distress, and afterwards happy even to transport as she stood behind the weak screen of muslin which protected her against the fascinating object she was contemplating. She felt a strong inclination to raise the curtain still higher; then again she experienced a kind of remorse at having raised it so high as it was; and finally the voice of conscientious devotion, heretofore so respectfully listened to, cried out:—" Beware, child! Pause before it is too late !"

Whilst caution whispered those words in one ear, love approached the other in powerful, eloquent and irresistible form. Its argument too must have been very strong, since it completely silenced the menacing voice of conscience.

After the lapse of a few moments, as might have been expected, what she doubtless desired took place. When Mr. Armstrong's reverie came to an end his eye naturally returned in the direction of the windows opposite.

Now we can safely affirm that Caroline would fain have concealed herself again had it been possible to do so on the instant. She abruptly drew the muslin curtain towards herself, but in doing so it caught in some object which prevented it from falling, and thus the young girl remained exposed to view opposite the handsome dreamer, who contemplated her beautiful features with enthusiastic delight.

" Caroline !" exclaimed the voice of Mrs. Dawson. The young girl, however, did not appear to hear her aunt's call.

Mr. Armstrong regarded her with a look which being interpreted meant,—

" I love you more dearly, and passionately, than it is impossible to describe !"

" Caroline !" exclaimed David in his turn.

The young girl, however, did not appear to understand, but stood in a state of intoxicated delight. Her heart seemed to leap towards the handsome cavalier opposite, who was now appealing to her by gestures as eloquent as they were polite. Two scalding tears trembled on the eyelashes of the young girl and fell down her beautiful cheeks.

" Ah !" she mentally exclaimed ; " he loves me, then !"

The handsome dreamer, who now saw his triumph, placed his fingers to his lips and threw a kiss across the court. This time the obstacle gave way, and the curtain fell. At the same moment two doors which opened into the room were abruptly thrust back.

" Caroline ! Caroline !" cried the united voices of Mrs. Dawson and her son, who both entered at the same time.

The young girl trembled violently, for she feared her secret would be detected.

" What are you doing there, my child ?" enquired Mrs. Dawson, with affectionate solicitude.

" There is something very interesting here, I presume, cousin," observed David, somewhat sharply ; " and it must be extremely attractive to prevent your hearing either my voice or that of your aunt."

The young girl blushed, stammered, and was unable to reply. David, who had always his jealous suspicions about him, rushed towards the window, for the purpose of raising the curtain to ascertain if he had judged correctly. Caroline, however, endeavoured to prevent him by a suppliant gesture, which added to his jealousy, and made him persevere ; he therefore took no notice of that mute appeal, but quickly raised the curtain.

Mrs. Dawson and her son thereupon looked eagerly about the court for a solution of the mystery, but, as Caroline had joyously observed, nothing could be seen. There was no longer any one at the windows of the first floor at the mysterious house, the thick silk curtains of whose casements were closely drawn together.

Notwithstanding she had ascertained that she was thus far secure from detection, Caroline naturally felt embarrassed. She respired with difficulty, and became somewhat alarmed at the increasing perplexity of her cousin, who gave vent to his feelings in an exclamation of anger. With regard to Mrs. Dawson, it required something infinitely more serious than that to trouble the amiable equanimity of her temper.

Mr. Armstrong had quitted his place at the moment when Caroline had again contrived to conceal herself behind the refractory curtain. He rose with the air of a man whom play begins to fatigue, and pulled the ornamental rope of a bell.

The little negro immediately appeared.

" Go and strike the gong in the centre hall," said Mr. Armstrong, as he referred to several items in his memorandum book.

" How many times, my lord ?"

" Five !"

The little negro departed through a different door to that which gave entrance to Black Bob.

A few seconds afterwards five dull and prolonged sounds were heard in the direction followed by the little negro. Mr. Armstrong took the same route on leaving his boudoir. He entered a handsome room of a circular form, which, as near as one could guess, was exactly in the centre of the large mysterious house. That apartment had no windows, but was lighted by an enormous sconce whenever required.

It was better provided with doors, however, for there were six, which seemed placed at equal distances from each other. Five of these opened on the spiral stairs, and it was by the sixth that Mr. Armstrong entered.

As he arrived the gong was still sending forth its sonorous, profound, and undulating vibrations. There was no one present in that mysterious apartment.

Five chairs, and a most magnificent couch or cushioned seat, were arranged round a vast stove, whose open mouth gave warmth and cheerfulness to the scene around it.

Mr. Armstrong carelessly threw himself on the cushioned seat. At the same moment five doors were opened. The two first, which opened in the direction of the brokers offices, gave passage to a lady richly attired, and a gentleman of fashionable appearance. The third, which opened towards Upper Thames Street, gave admittance to a gentleman of honest mien, and who was dressed as a merchant. Through the fourth came a little thin man with a yellowish physiognomy, and whose costume seemed accustomed to the sharp context with his pointed joints. Finally, the fifth gave passage to Mr. Matthews, adorned with his green spectacles and enormous half-mask.

The lady came from the sumptuous and extensive costume warehouse, of which she was the real sovereign and mistress.

The gentleman, who entered at the same time, was Mr. Johnson, her neighbour, the jeweller.

The gentleman with the honest look, was Mr. Mole, the bill broker and money changer.

Finally, the fourth was no less a personage than the old Robert Roll, an elderly ruined attorney, who studied the evasion rather than the practice of law, in the sale of trinkets and curiosities at his gloomy shop in Mint Lane.

Of these five personages, Mrs. Thompson and Mr. Robert Roll, were the only two who exhibited their physiognomies as nature had formed them. That was very unfortunate for the poor attorney, for he had all the appearance of being a cunning old usurer; on the other hand, it was all the better for the lady, as she was still very beautiful, and it enabled her to exhibit her charms to the utmost advantage.

The other three wore that kind of mask which most suited his taste and the fashion of the period.

Thus, Mr. Matthews had a half-mask; and Mr. Mole agreed with his taste in the use of green spectacles, to which the latter added a large black peruke, that slightly contrasted with the light colour of his whiskers. Mr. Johnson, the jeweller, on the contrary, had blue cheeks, which did not, however, prevent him from sporting fine dark moustaches, and a head of hair of the same hue splendidly crisped.

All this might have seemed very correct and judicious; there was nothing very extraordinary or remarkable therein.

It is probable that the sight of Mr. Matthews was rather weak, as also that of Mr. Mole, who had learned to fancy dark hair. With regard to Mr. Johnson and his borrowed peruke, we may safely affirm that every hair-dresser in London must have failed, had it been no longer fashionable for the young dandies of town to wear magnificent wigs and fine curling moustaches.

Be that as it may, however, the five individuals who had just replied to the call of the little negro, advanced with a cautious step towards Mr. Armstrong, and respectfully saluted him.

The latter warmly pressed the hand of Mrs. Thompson, and bowed his acknowledgments to the others.

Mrs. Thompson immediately sat down, but the four gentlemen remained standing till a royal gesture from Mr. Armstrong, the leading member of the firm, as it would seem, permitted them to be seated.

Now, if Mrs. Brown, Mrs. Green, or Mrs. Blue, could but have glanced through brick walls, and observed that scene, with what joyous exultation she would have summoned Mrs. White, to relate the particulars of the whole affair! And how jealous they would have rendered Mrs. Blood and her neighbours of Bury-street!

After the singular and mysterious congress had sat some minutes in silence, Mr. Armstrong raised himself, referred to his embroidered memorandum book, and again resumed his musing attitude, apparently unconscious of the presence of his partners. At length, however, he put his hand to his pocket, from whence he drew a splendid gold watch, enriched with diamonds.

"Half-past twelve," he murmured; "am I right, Johnson?"

"You are perfectly right, my Lord,'

"Then I have not much time to devote to you. Let us therefore come to the point at once; I require ten thousand pounds."

"Ten thousand pounds!" exclaimed Robert Rolls with profound astonishment.

"Ten thousand!" repeated in chorus the money changer, the jeweller, and Mrs. Thompson, the costumier.

"For this evening," added Mr. Armstrong, coldly.

Every eye was lowered at once, and a dark shade appeared to be gathering on the countenance of all.

"Mr. Mole," resumed the principal, "can you let me have it at once?"

"I can, my Lord, but ———"

"But what?"

"It must be in such money as you do not desire, I apprehend."

"Nay, that is useless in the present case. What have you to say, Mr. Johnson?"

" Business is deplorably bad, my Lord."

" And you, Julia?" interrupted Mr. Armstrong, addressing Mrs. Thompson.

" My cash box is at your disposal, my Lord," replied the beautiful costumier; " but it does not contain anything like that amount."

" I will take what there is, Julia. You are a charming creature. And you, Mr. Roll?"

" I will tell your Lordship," replied the old lawyer; " I will tell you frankly, and without ambages; I am sorry I can only repeat what my worthy neighbour Mr. Johnson said—business is very bad, and I may even add that it is at a stand still."

" Well, Mr. Roll, what is to be done?"

" My case, such as it is—and God knows that it is by no means well filled—is at your Lordship's disposal."

" No," replied Mr. Armstrong, after a moment's consideration. " As to you, Mr. Matthews," he afterwards added, " I know what you have. Upon my word, gentlemen, this is very bad; you surely must be sleeping, for every time that I ask you for a trifle ———"

" Ten thousand pounds!" sighed Robert Roll.

" You are always introducing interminable lamentations," pursued his Lordship with increased vexation. " It is becoming intolerable! Are you kept without merchandise? On the contrary, have you not an abundant quantity? Do the authorities interfere with your mercantile transactions? Have not the whole of the fashionable world learned to send to your warehouses? And to whom, pray, are you indebted for all this? Merchandise! security! reputation! It is *I* who gave you all this, and yet you seem loth to acknowledge it in a satisfactory manner."

" God forbid!" exclaimed Johnson.

" You know, my Lord, that I am willing to serve you to the best of my ability," murmured Mrs. Thompson.

" I know it, and thank you heartily, Julia. But these gentlemen—"

" We are prepared," interrupted Mr. Johnson.

" Yes, we are ready, my lord," repeated Mr. Roll, who added, between his teeth, " but I protest in all due form against such tyranic demands as these."

" Very good!" replied his lordship, rising; " I rely on you for this evening. In return, rely on me and fear nothing; I will protect you against trouble and danger. Adieu, Julia."

Mrs. Thompson recrossed the threshold of the door by which she had entered, and which conducted her to the costume warehouse, and each of the three others led to one of the shops on the ground floor. The fifth communicated with the offices of Armstrong & Co., as we have already seen.

" Have you anything to say to me, Mr. Johnson?" demanded his lordship.

Nothing, except your affair of to-night," replied the jeweller, smiling.

" As usual, on that head, Johnson, as usual. That will not trouble us long."

" So much the better, my lord. To whom shall I remit my portion of the fund?"

" As usual, to Mrs. Thompson."

Mr. Johnson then departed, bowing.

" I have some bad news for your lordship," observed the bill-broker, as soon as the door was closed. They refused three of our bank notes yesterday; and what is worse, there are unpleasant rumours afloat in the city.

" What is said, then?"

" Nothing precise and definite at present; but there are discussions of an unfavourable character, and everybody seems to be distrustful. People will no longer take one of our bank notes without turning it over twenty times in a suspicious manner."

" Is that all? Be not apprehensive, Mole, my friend," said Mr. Armstrong; " before long I will give the bank notes which none will refuse! You may retire, my dear friend."

The stock-broker traversed the room with measured steps, and disappeared through the door which opened on the staircase leading to his office.

Mr. Matthews then walked softly round the room, and partly opened each door in order to see that no intrusive listener remained behind. After that he returned to his chief.

" Friend Matthews," said the latter, " you must be more prudent for the future, and not make use of the pistol till the last extremity. It is a noisy weapon at least, and may create unpleasant disturbances here. In our terrene paradise amidst the Welsh mountains it is different. But we have said enough on that subject. I myself saw that you were closely pressed, and felt it necessary to appear before the matter went further. I believe, from what I then saw, that those men will not refuse our bank notes."

" That is according to circumstances," replied Mr. Matthews. " Our *contractors*," continued the latter, with a significant emphasis on the last word, " must take all without hesitation or distrust. Your Highness's body-guard in the country, however, will only take gold. They are the most intractable brigands I have ever heard of."

" I like them all the better for that! But tell me about the affair in Prince's-street. How do your mining operations proceed?"

[We deem it necessary to inform the reader in this place, that the street alluded to by Mr. Armstrong was one which ran along one side of the Bank.]

"I was there this morning," resumed Mr. Matthews. "Captain Cable urges his giant on as fast as he possibly can. He gorges him with beef, and saturates him with ale, by which means the mighty fellow does more work than any ten men could perform in the same time."

"It is, nevertheless. too long in operation," said Mr. Armstrong with a sigh of chagrin.

"Prince's-street is thirty feet wide," replied Mr. Matthews; "and our elephant digs twenty feet deep; but another eighteen or twenty feet will accomplish the business."

"Thank God for that, Matthews!" exclaimed the chief. "Then your cash-box will be filled in reality!"

Mr. Armstrong then arose from his cushioned seat, and thrust his white fingers into a pair of perfumed gloves. He then touched a spring which communicated by means of wires with the outer apartment, and proceeded towards the door.

"Good morning," said he. "Pray see that old Robert Roll performs his duty this evening. Every time that I ask him for a trifle it seems almost to break his heart. But I must positively have ten thousand this evening."

Mr. Armstrong took the staircase which led towards Mr. Johnson's, the jewellers, and remained with him a few minutes apparently for the purpose of choosing some articles from his abundant stock. He then departed as one who had been making purchases, leaped into a magnificent equipage drawn by a pair of beautiful horses, whose equals, perhaps, were not to be found in England; not even, probably, in the matchless stables of the Duke de Duro.

Scarcely had he thrown himself on the soft cushions of the carriage, when the horses set off at a rapid gallop towards the fashionable quarters in the west end.

—o—

CHAPTER XII.

BLACK BOB AND HIS PROCEEDINGS.

After leaving the house of Armstrong & Co., Black Bob proceeded along the dirty pavement of Cheapside, and continued his course towards the neighbourhood of St. Giles's. That delicate and worthy fellow did not hesitate to push females and children out of his way, as he proceeded along; but when, perchance, a gentleman or lady-like personage appeared, he roughly hastened to clear a passage for them.

Black Bob proceeded through the fog with an agility which did not seem in keeping with the usual apathy of his movements. He was not long in traversing the space which separated Mint Lane from that labyrinth of passages and courts, which bear the name of St. Giles. On arriving in the latter neighbourhood, he passed down a narrow tortuous lane, where the atmosphere became so dense and dark by the thickened fog mixing with the foul vapours which incessantly issued from the low cells and sinks of that filthy district.

He stopped before an old worm-eaten door, whose frame seemed bound with rusty hoop-iron. The dwelling into which he entered, like almost the whole of those in the foul neighbourhood, had only two floors in addition to its cellarage. Master Bob did not reside on the ground-floor, neither did he inhabit the first, but passed down a few steps into an apartment which looked very much like a cave.

As he descended, a warm, heavy vapour enveloped him; fetid smells filled his chest, and acted so powerfully, that another would have revolted, or, perhaps have been suffocated thereby. Black Bob, however, received those exhalations as a horse inhales the odour of its stable, or a Common Councilman the rich perfumes of Smithfield and its sewers. He made a grunt of satisfaction; felt his pockets in order to re-assure himself that his pecularum was secure from the dangers of his journey, and raised the latch of a door which gave entrance to his singularly obscure dwelling, heated to an extraordinary degree by an enormous stove, crammed full with coke.

"Confound thee, Steady," said he on entering, "what, in the ruffin's name hast been a doin' on? I'll be d—d if ye vont burn yerself to death, like a old sot as thee be'st!"

No one replied; and the only sounds which were heard in the room issued from the reddened stove, which was snoring like a forge.

"Steady!" exclaimed Bob; "Steady, I say! Vill ye answer me, ye cursed—"

Black Bob interrupted himself in the midst of his passionate exclamations in consequence of having approached a body that lay sprawling near the corner, and which seemed to join in a snoring duet with the heated stove. After drawing the apparently inanimate mass of humanity towards the fire, and for an instant contemplating it with an air of vexation, he took it roughly by the arm, which he vigorously shook several times. In a few moments the hoarse voice of the prostrate figure muttered, with the dull, irregular muttering of a drunken person.

"Another drop, plase! only one go more, good

Mrs. Mixture! I'm werry thusty, and it's Black Bob as pays for it."

Bob bounded like a tiger to a certain part of the room, which we shall visit by and bye; but, having apparently satisfied himself that all was right in that quarter, returned to the inert object before the fire.

"Anoth—er drop," repeated the figure.

"I'll give it ye directly, ye—" commenced Bob, with the grin of a tiger. He was interrupted, however, by the figure.

"Thank'ee, Mrs. Mix—; Bob pay—s!"

"She's as drunk as a pipe of porter!" exclaimed the latter, in an angry tone. "Steady, ye cursed vitch! Steady, I say!"

Steady, which seemed to be the name of the figure, did not move an inch. Finding a simple call ineffectual, Black Bob poured on the devoted head of poor Steady a volume of oaths that were enough to have aroused Satan himself.

"Hang it," he muttered, "she mustn't lie there. I must see if I can't wake her up somehow. Ah, I have it!"

He thereupon seized the red hot bar of iron which served the purposes of a poker, and applied it to the nostrils of the prostrate Steady. The latter started violently as the heated metal touched her face, raised herself up, and after several ineffectual efforts, at length staggered to her feet.

She was a tall, powerful-looking woman, about forty-five years of age. Her countenance seemed bloated and hectic, which, with two red eyes, denoted the favourite passion.

"I'm very thirsty," she observed in a hoarse voice, as she fixed on Bob an earnest and inquiring glance.

"Thirsty be ye? Werry good!" replied the latter, as he brandished his heated poker; "thirsty, ye infernal toper! while I'm obleeged to work all day, you like to be smothered in drink. But I'll be d—d if ye shant vork too, or not a spot of drink touches yer lips agin, ye ———! May the ruffin smash me, Steady, if I don't dash thy brains out agin the wall some fine night, ye dirty sot!"

Notwithstanding the brutal energy of these menaces, there was a kind of tenderness in the voice of Bob while thus giving vent to his passionate vexation.

"Ah! ah! my pretty Bob," hickuped the tall woman; "let's have 'nother drop—don't ye see as how my throat's a burnin'?"

Steady had, by some extraordinary process peculiar to those who are thoroughly intoxicated, diagonally made the tour round the stove, and mechanically approached a table whereon were placed a gin bottle and drinking horn, both of which were empty.

"Not a drop," she murmured ill-humouredly, "my pretty Bob! hastn't thee a George in thy fob for yer little voman?"

"A George, ye ———! No! Half-a-crown is more than I gets arter a whole day's beggin', sometimes. If ye vonts so much tin, vhy don't ye turn out as a honest mendicant should. But I'll be d—d if ye shall have any more tin from me!"

"I'm thirsty," interrupted Steady, who had again squatted down behind the stove for the purpose of having another nap.

"I must get rid on her somehow," muttered Bob; "for if she sees me go to ———"

Master Bob suddenly interrupted himself, and for a few minutes remained in what is popularly termed "a brown study." At length he turned towards his amiable partner with a look of anxiety.

"Steady!" he again cried in a loud voice; "hang it if I can refuse thee anything, my vench; come, here's a bob for ye to goo and treat yerself to some more gin!"

This time Mrs. Steady arose without the aid of a red-hot poker, staff, or any thing else, and bounded to the side of her indulgent husband with a rapidity that literally astounded him. Such is the power of money!

"A bob! only a bob? Can't ye gi' us another, my pretty?"

Black Bob frowned severely, and raised his poker in a menacing manner; but Steady, whom the idea of inhaling two or three more horns of gin had rendered agile, immediately ascended the stairs, singing merrily as she proceeded.

Bob followed her closely to the street door, which he closed after her. That done, he returned to his cave, the door of which he carefully barricaded.

"Is it possible that sich a jewell of a voman as her should be so werry fond of spendin' money?" muttered Bob whilst lighting his lamp at the stove. "She is five feet six in height!" he continued, in a tone of admiration; and sich a colour, too! May the ruffin take me if one mayn't travel all through St. Giles's, Holborn, and the whole city without finding her equal! May the thunder strike me if there aint many great lords as would be glad to have her for their lady! Five foot six! And talkin' of Lords, my bisniss the other Sunday evening vill be useful more vays nor one. The Marquiss is a first-rate judge of vomen, and that little mendicant of the church is the most suiterble girl —not for me, though; for I likes tall, fine vomen —but for the gentry vho likes valkin' about vith mistusses only five foot!"

Bob smiled with contempt at the idea of admiring a female so short; he however directed his steps towards one of the corners of his obscure apartment.

"I shall have a nice bait for the Marquis of Minchington in that little mendicant of the church," he continued; "and if he bites vell, it'll be a fifty-meg job for me; perhaps more! That'll be just the ticket, for times is very bad, and folks vont drop their tin as they used to do. Then, there's Steady, who drinks like a fish; but it must be admitted she's a extraordinary fine voman!"

After carefully examining the wall for a moment, Black Bob touched one of the stones, which immediately yielded to the pressure of his finger.

"Ve don't see vomen five feet six high every day," he added.

The stone moved at its base, swung for an instant, and then slipped on one side, leaving to view an open space of about one foot square. Bob hastily plunged his head aft r the lamp into the aperture, and remained in that position for several minutes. He did not utter a single word, but an avidious and eager delight caused his small eyes to sparkle beneath their dark lashes. He now placed his lamp on the ground, and went to the door in order to satisfy himself that he was free from interruption.

Then in two bounds he regained the hole, and eagerly plunged his right hand therein. His whole body seemed agitated, and an unusual smile lighted up his gloomy features as the sound of gold was heard in the aperture.

At first he handled his treasure delicately, as one caresses a beloved object; then he would grasp whole handfuls with the joy of a miser; muttering incoherent sentences as his fingers penetrated the accumulated hoard.

We cannot say, precisely, what amount that original description of cash-box contained; but the hole seemed deep, and sometimes the arms of Bob disappeared to the very elbow in the precious metal which was secreted there. Occasionally he would withdraw whole handfuls, hold them at arms-length with an air of enthusiastic delight, and then throw them back noisily among the rest.

When he had fully satiated himself with the sight and examination of his treasure, he drew from his pocket the seven guineas which he had received in the house of Armstrong and Co., and placed them with the others.

"Oh, ye little darlings!" he exclaimed; "it vos nice and varm in my pocket for ye! Lie still, I'll come and see ye agin afore long! Ye shall go into the country if I'm lucky."

He took "a last fond look" of his precious treasure, from which he had a great deal of difficulty in separating himself. At length, after having

hesitated for some time, he replaced the stone so adroitly that the most experienced eye could not have distinguished it from the others.

"Steady is uncommon cunnin' vhen sober; but then, she's almost al'ys drunk! and it strikes me I'm a deuced sight more artful than her! Besides," he added, taking down his barricade, "isn't it as much for her I vorks as meself?"

A few minutes afterwards Bob issued from the door, and again saw the daylight,—at least the thick fog which filled the lane. In a dirty tavern, a few steps from his door, he perceived his amiable companion, Steady, who was sleeping soundly with her head on the table.

"Vhat a pity!" he growled, in a tone of regret; "a voman five foot six!"

He again set out on a new excursion at a pace as rapid as he came, and passed through thoroughfares with the speed of locomotion. As he issued from the narrow passage in which his dwelling was situated, the neighbouring church clock struck two.

After passing through a number of streets, lanes, and courts, he finally arrived at Woburn-terrace, and stopped before a large mansion, whose front, according to custom, was defended by iron palisading.

On each side of the door-steps, several valets, grooms, and other servants were standing and merrily conversing together. Black Bob placed his foot on the first step, and was about to ascend the others, when a little fellow in the guise of a jockey called out,

"What does that black-looking rascal want here?"

"What, Master Foot," replied Bob; "don't ye know me then?"

"Some mendicant, I calculate?"

"Ah!" exclaimed one of the valets; "it's Black Bob, the beauty of St. Giles's!"

"Yes," added Bob; "I'm Bob Bantam, of St. Giles's, at yer sarvice, gen'lemen."

"Oh! ah! very good!" exclaimed two or three of the grooms; "Black Bob, the husband of the lovely Mrs. Steady!"

"Well, what dost want here?"

"I vonts to see me lord's steward, if it ain't unpossible."

"He is engaged, and can't be seen now, my fine fellow," observed the valet on duty.

"But I'se got some special news for Mr. Ledger, as he vonts to know; besides, him and me be old acquaintances, so he'll be glad to see me, I'm sure."

"Oh! oh! oh! Old acquaintances, eh!" rejoined the valet, ironically; "that alters the case! Make way for Master Bob! Make way, that I may announce the gentleman!"

9

"I hope ye'll grant us your powerful protection," said a groom, laughing.

"Don't forget me," added the little jockey.

"Nor me," continued a third; "or I shall wait upon Mrs. Steady, the beauty of St. Giles's, to secure her interest in my behalf."

"At yer sarvice, gen'lemen; at yer sarvice;" repeated Black Bob, without relaxing for a moment his humble smile.

Bob Bantam was a prudent man, as his conduct in this trying scene abundantly testified. The valet at once preceded him with an affected air to the upper apartments of the mansion.

"You'll have to wait some time, my noble friend," said the former, tittering; "for there's a great many persons waiting in Mr. Ledger's antechamber for an interview."

"No matter, Mr. Pumps, no matter," repeated Bob; "if I must vait, vhy I s'pose I must, and there's an end of the bisniss; for under any sarcumstances its unpossible I can go back agin vithout seein' on him."

There was, indeed, a numerous group in the waiting-room of Mr. Ledger. Amongst them were five or six tradesmen, who had come for a settlement of their claims, some of which were of long standing; several persons whose costumes and physiognomies denoted that they were either country officials, or dependants of the house; and many who appeared to be candidates for, rather than the recipients of, patronage.

The valet partly opened Mr. Ledger's door, and announced the name of Bantam.

The poor fellows who had doubtless been waiting there for several hours, directed eager glances through the aperture of the door, in order to ascertain who was the vexatious personage whose prolonged visit had so mercilessly barred the threshhold of the steward's room. They gazed with all their might, and were exceedingly mortified to find that there was no one present except Mr. Ledger himself, who seemed comfortably occupied in picking his teeth, whilst reclining in an arm chair before the fire, with his large feet resting on the fender. The tradesmen, dependants, and others, however, fancied that they did not see all.

"Bantam?" repeated Mr. Ledger, without turning round — I don't know—eh?—ah!—Bantam—the devil—oh! Who is Bantam?"

"It's me, please yer honor," replied Bob, who endeavoured to advance.

After us, man, after us," cried the united voices of all present.

"I think that voice seems familiar," muttered Mr. Ledger. "Yes, it must be the worthy kidnapper of St. Giles's!"

A loud murmur was raised in the waiting-room, where the assemblage seemed determined to prevent the further progress of Black Bob.

"My good gen'lemen," commenced Bob, with his usual humility when speaking to his superiors —but a display of eloquence was not required, for the moment that the valet received an order to show Bob into the steward's room, he caught up a long wet broom, with which he stepped forward and violently distributed a shower of dirty water, both right and left. The group precipitately retreated, loudly grumbling as they did so, and Bob hastened to follow the passage thus marked out for him.

"Close the door," said Mr. Ledger, who still sat immovable before the fire.

Bob immediately closed the door.

"Come hither," continued the steward.

Mr. Ledger appeared a middle-aged man, somewhat corpulent, with a large round face, in the centre of which shone a prodigious nose, whose colour seemed to vie with the fire that warmed it. His physiognomy, on the whole, expressed an apathetic coldness, almost brutal. His eyes were grey, and of an ordinary expression; but his small, flat mouth, by a certain habit of twitching, spoke enough of itself.

On entering the apartment of Mr. Ledger, Bob looked all round to see if any other persons were present, but there was no one except the steward himself, whose only object in keeping so many waiting, seemed to be the exercise of his own pleasure, and the proper use of his toothpick.

After the lapse of a few minutes—during which he concluded the process of cleaning his teeth, swallowed two glasses of wine, and took a pinch of snuff—he raised his eyes on Bob.

"You have something for sale, I presume," said he, smiling sarcastically.

"Sir?"

"Some bargain, eh? You understand!" continued the steward, with something like a wink.

Bob began to grin.

"Vot yer honor seys is the werry thing," he muttered; "it is some'ot good!"

"You have come at a very unfortunate time, for the goods are not so much in demand just now. His lordship does not require any more at present."

"But these be some'ot more splendacious than common," observed Bob.

"Come again, my fine fellow."

"It's unpossible, yer honor, seein' as how such goods as them von't keep long!" added Bob, with a satanic chuckle.

"Are they very beautiful, then?" demanded the steward.

"Werry!" replied Bob, with a grin; "she's as beautiful as a hangel! The devil take me if I thinks there is any hangels half so bewitching!"

Mr. Ledger took another glass of wine, and a pinch of snuff—rubbed his nose, and gazed at the fire.

"Very pretty, eh?"

"Yer honor can see her, if ye likes."

"What would be the utility of it? His lordship is already satiated, and I can therefore see no use of such a proceeding, my worthy Bob Blackem."

"Bob Bantam, if so be as it pleases yer honor; my name's Bantam. Ah! my lord is werry—but p'rhaps I ain't rightly understood ye?"

"I will explain it to you then, my *honest* fellow! Have you ever eaten more roast beef than your stomach could well contain?"

"Werry seldom, yer honor; bisniss is werry bad—indeed, it's devilish hard to get a livin' anyhow."

"No matter whether that has been the case but seldom or frequently, if you admit that you were at least once satiated with beef."

"You means, yer honor, I didn't want no more?"

"Precisely," rejoined Mr. Ledger, with a smile; "neither does my lord require any more angels!—I see we understand each other now."

"Howsomever, its werry strange to me! Vhy, accordin' to that, yer honor, my vife, Steady, ought to ha' been *satcheated* vith gin long ago! But it's a great pity for his lordship, seein' as how sich a jewel isn't found every day! Howsomever, I'm sorry for havin' troubled yer honor."

Black Bob made a low bow, and proceeded towards the door; but, just as he was about to open it, the voice of Mr. Ledger recalled him therefrom.

"What is her age?" he inquired, with feigned indifference.

"About seventeen, or p'rhaps eighteen, yer honor. Ah! ye should only see her! My eyes!—isn't she a duck! Vhy, she's as fresh as a daisy, and as gentle as a lamb!"

"Indeed!" exclaimed the steward; "where, then, does she reside?"

"That's the werry thing I'm come about," replied Bob, with an ignoble smile; "the number of the street is half the bisniss; but then ye seys as how his lordship is—I forgets the vord, but it seems he is as I vos vhen I had too much beef."

"Listen, Bill," resumed Mr. Ledger.

"Bob, if it please yer honor."

"Well, then, my dear Bob Bunting—"

"Bob Bantam, my name is, yer honor."

"No matter whether Bob, Bill, Jack, Joe, or Jem, my honest fellow; but, do not interrupt me

again. Let us make another attempt. If she be as beautiful as you have described—"

"Ten thousan' times more beautiful!"

"Perhaps his lordship could not see without loving her?"

"I'll be d—d if he could!"

"We must try him."

"That's jist vot I think's, yer honor."

"There's another reason why I should be moving, and that is, since the marriage of his son, my lord has very much changed his mode of life, by which my influence is getting weak. Would you believe it, his lordship has been inquiring very particularly into the state of my accounts!!"

Bob appeared to be perfectly astounded by that intelligence.

"Unpossible!" said he, seriously.

"It is but too true; therefore it is time I should adopt some measure for directing his attention into another channel. Yes, I must seek that young girl."

"Werry good."

"I'll see her very soon."

"Werry good."

"What do you require for your services?"

Bob quietly proceeded towards the fire-place, and coolly placed his elbow on the mantle-piece.

"I'll give ye her name and all perticklars, if ye'll count down to me thirty guineas," he slowly whispered.

"You are mad, Bob!"

"Not a bit of it."

"Thirty guineas for an address!"

"And all perticklers about the prettiest girl in London."

"But, thirty guineas!"

"It's a mere trifle under the sarcumstarnces."

"Allow me to differ with you there, my honest friend."

"When you've seen her, you'll say to yerself, 'Vot a fool that Bob Bantam is; vhy, she's vorth a hundred guineas!'"

"Some one else may have seen this young lady."

"That may be, but it's no use if they have."

Mr. Ledger reflected a moment; after which he rose, and without saying one word, proceeded towards his closet, whilst Bob watched him with an avidious look.

The steward opened one of the drawers, and took therefrom a quantity of gold. He then relocked the closet, and counted down the thirty guineas which Bob had demanded.

"The terms are very exorbitant," he murmured, "but that rascal has never yet deceived me. He is the most adroit kidnapper in London, and seems purposely created for this kind of business. Besides, it is his lordship who pays for it after all! Come hither," he continued, in a higher tone; "if you deceive me now—"

"Ah! ah!" chuckled Bob; "yer honor's a joking, I'm sure. It ain't likely I'd run the risk of losing so good a customer for sich a trifle."

"Here, take this," observed Mr. Ledger, pointing to the money.

Bob did not require a second invitation, but eagerly seized the gold, which disappeared as if by enchantment, into the vast recesses of his pocket.

"Thanks, her honor thanks," he pursued; "and now I'll give ye the perticklers, if ye'll take 'em down. Caroline Jones, number 7, Watling-square, Mint Lane. There be two sisters, a old aunt or mother, and a young man who must be either a brother or a cousin."

"I don't like the young man," grumbled Mr. Ledger.

"It's awkard, sartainly; but in case of need, I'm al'ys ready to undertake these sort of things," said Bob, making an atrocious and significant gesture, which it would have been impossible to misunderstand; at the same time he exhibited by way of illustration, the enormous knife to which we have already alluded.

"I understand," said the steward with a shudder.

"Yes," continued Bob, "this pretty thing has silenced many a one, and is likely enough to do for as many more yet."

A smile, at once diabolical and exulting, was perceptible on his repulsive features, as he uttered those frightful words. The steward felt uneasy, although he managed to appear calm.

"You must have made thousands in your time, my worthy fellow," remarked the steward, after a moment's silence.

"Me! not so easy. Bisniss is devilish bad, and it's hard to get a livin' anyhow. Indeed, I ain't got a copper more nor the thirty guineas yer honor's just give me. Good day to yer honor! May God bless ye. I'll call again soon and see if yer honor vants anythin' in my vay. If that young feller puts ye to any trouble, let me know, and—and——Good bye yer honor."

"Stay," said the steward, reflecting a moment; "you had better call again to-morrow."

"Werry good, yer honor," replied Bob. "Is there anything else ye've got to say afore I goes?"

"No."

Good day, yer honor," repeated Bob, bowing humbly as he departed. The creditors, dependants, and others, regarded him as he passed with a sort of morose envy. He, however, proceeded through the waiting room, saluting them on every side, amidst murmurs of increasing impatience.

After he had left the steward's bell rang, and a valet attended. In a few moments the latter returned, and announced to those assembled in the ante-chamber that Mr. Ledger could not possibly receive any one till the next day.

"This is a decent piece of bisniss," muttered Bantam to himself, as he once more appeared in the open street. "I'll give Steady another bob to-night."

He slowly continued his route, without any immediate object in view, save that of acting so generously towards his amiable partner, whose superior charms seemed to occupy all his idle moments, for he once more repeated with enthusiasm—"Five foot six! Five foot six!"

Presently a gentleman stopped him as he was returning towards Mint-lane. Bob, however, seemed still so much occupied in the contemplation of his superb "five foot six" of flesh, that he had no time for thinking about tin, and accordingly endeavoured to pass onwards; but the gentleman arrested his progress by a gesture, and said, with a strong French accent, "Can you direct me to St. Paul's?"

"It's a fine place," replied Bob coldly.

"No doubt; but will you be good enough to inform me where it is?"

"That's rather difficult," replied Bob.

"Why I understood it was near this place."

"Indeed!" exclaimed the avaricious mendicant in a tone of surprise; but always having an eye to business of any kind, he resumed,—"I'll show ye the way for two bob."

"What is two bob?"

"I mean two shillins'."

"Two shillings for a single word?"

"Vell, I'll do it for von, then, since you ain't a Russian, Prussian, nor Spanian, Mr. Frenchman."

Bob thereupon extended his open hand, into which the stranger placed a shilling, muttering in an undertone a few words touching English hospitality, that were by no means flattering.

Vell, my lord duke, continued Bob, with exquisite coolness, "if ye vants St. Paul's, ye've only to valk for'ard as straight as this crooked street vill take ye, and at the other end on it ye'll find St. Paul's chuchhard. It ain't a quarter of a mile!—Good day!"

The stranger muttered something in French, then turned on his heel and proceeded in the direction indicated to him.

Although rather clever in his way, Black Bob was not capable of replying to the observation of the stranger, pronounced in a foreign language; he, consequently, took no further notice thereof, but hastened forward, and mixed with the crowd.

"Now," said he to himself, "shall I go and sell the guvnor's name to that young man? I should get a good price, that's clear!" Then, after a few moments' reflection, he resumed, "No, that vont do at no price! It vould cause suxspicion, and prewent bisniss from goin' on comfortably." After another slight pause, he continued, "Ah, ah, ah! Mr. Ledger has made a nice bargain! Vhy, the guvnor vill have nailed that young girl afore the steward has time to say 'Jack Robinson!' That's his bisniss, not mine, though I got thirty guineas for it!"

The worthy Bob, upon second consideration, did not pursue his route towards Mint Lane, but turned back in the direction of his own dwelling, and, as he proceeded, employed his thoughts in devising some new scheme of operation for the night. He was a rare fellow for "bisniss."

"This evenin'," thought he, "I'll go and see my pals the backed-pullers (resurrectionists) and stiffiners (burkers). Their bisniss is rather unpleasant, and the pay ain't by no means good: but then, a body must get a livin' somehow. Talking of that, blow me if this ain't a fine day for the good old trade of beggin'!"

The latter idea seemed to strike him in consequence of observing several persons bestow alms on a mendicant, who was mounted on a frame by the side of an organ, of which he seemed to form a part.

As Bob proceeded homewards, however, he began to calculate how much money he had made during the day; and having ascertained, by dint of repeated applications to his fingers, that the amount was rather considerable, came to the resolution of retiring from "bisniss" for the remainder of the evening. That night, too, he seemed to be filled with tender sentiments towards his beloved "five foot six," who had never before appeared so handsome in his eyes.

"I'll see the stiffiners another night," said he to himself; "it ain't been a bad day, not by no means, and, somehow, I'm a gettin' tired. I dare say Backer couldn't give me more nor two megs for a night's diggin' in some chuchhard. Two guineas is summut, sartainly, and ain't to be sneezed at in these times; for bisniss is werry bad, and—but Steady is vaitin' for me, I dare say, poor creetur. May the devil take me if I vouldn't give a guinea a'most if she'd only get drunk not more nor six times a veek!"

Bob now hastened onwards; he proceeded along Newgate Street, Holborn, and finally arrived at St. Giles's, where we will leave him for the present.

—o—

CHAPTER XIII.

SHOWS HOW "ONE MAN IN HIS TIME PLAYS MANY PARTS."

IT has been said by one of our most talented authors, that "the mendicants of London are the best actors in the world." Whether this may positively be true or not, we are unable to form an opinion, but that they are generally equal to any of the ordinary artists of our stage, few, we believe, can deny. In the course of our travels through the crowded streets of this mighty metropolis, we have met them in countless numbers and endless variety. Indeed, the different *characters* which the *professional* mendicant assumes in order to impose on unthinking and kindhearted people, is as great as it is sometimes amusing.

We do not propose, however, in this place to enter into a general dissertation on the genus *Mendicant*; on the contrary, our present chapter must be devoted to a faithful record of the "many parts" which Black Bob played in the course of a short time.

On the morning after that amiable and honest personage had returned from his visit to the Marquis of Minchington, he arose somewhat earlier than usual; that is to say, it was about nine o'clock.

"Steady, my vench!" cried Bob, as he drew over his "understandings" an article of dress which bore some slight resemblance to a pair of "unmentionables;" "Steady, I say! Well, I'm blest if I don't believe she's still as drunk as ever!"

After he had adjusted the said inexpressibles, Black Bob leaned over the straw mattrass on which his amiable partner lay, and gave her a rough shake.

"Another drop," muttered Steady in her sleep; "another—"

"Devil!" rejoined Bob.

"Drop!" preferred Steady.

"Not a spot!" returned Bob, who gave the worthy lady another shaking, which aroused her.

"Eh! ah! vot's the matter?" inquired Steady, rubbing her eyes.

"It's time to be moving, my old voman."

"Vots up?"

"Nothin' pertickler," only I'm goin' a maunderin' to-day, my vench; so look alive and get us some grub."

While his amiable partner was dressing, Master Bob relighted the coke which still remained in the large iron stove, and then sat musingly before it.

"I vonts some tin for the grub," observed Steady, holding out her hand at the same time.

Bob gave her two shillings, with which Mrs. Steady purchased a savoury breakfast. After their repast the worthy pair arose.

"Now for bisniss," observed Bob, approaching a large chest, from which he selected about twenty articles of dress.

"Vot's the calls ?"* enquired Steady.

"Salter, Redcoat, Skinner, and Dancer†," replied Bob, coldly; "or anythin' else as turns up."

The next two hours were fully occupied by the worthy couple in "dressing" Master Bob to "play his part." After selecting from a somewhat extensive wardrobe such articles as were deemed requisite, the latter threw them on the floor, seated himself in front of the fire, and began to take off the few clothes which he wore.

The first operation consisted in "making up" Master Bob as a cripple. His right leg was bent backwards at the knee, and strongly lashed in that position; indeed, so powerfully had Mrs. Steady exerted herself on this point, that the flesh of the upper and lower portions of the leg seemed kneaded together, and it would take a keen eye to detect the imposture. The left arm was treated in much the same manner; but doubled forwards, with the hand upon the shoulder. A large black patch covered one eye; and, finally, two streaks of light paint, admirably drawn by the faithful hand of Mrs. Steady, exquisitely depicted the seams of severe wounds on each cheek.

When this part of the dressing was completed, Bob took two or three hearty draughts of hot brandy that had been prepared as a stimulant against the pain which he thus voluntarily endured.

"Take a swig yerself, Steady," said Bob.

The lady did not require a second invitation to drink; but forthwith emptied the horn, and then replenished it.

"Here's luck to ye," she proposed as a toast, whilst tasting the newly brewed liquor.

"That 'll do," observed Bob, after taking a draught; "now help us on with them fleshins."

Mrs. Steady thereupon picked up a mysterious looking article that seemed made to fit the left leg and foot as tight as possible; its colour bore some slight resemblance to that of the human body; hence it probably derived the term of fleshings. This was drawn on with considerable difficulty, for it seemed much too small. Another article of a similar hue, was placed over the upper portion of the body. A pair of old grey trowsers were next produced, and carefully put on; these were surmounted by a tight soldier's jacket without any

tails. An old stock completed the first portion of our artiste's costume.

After spending a few moments in admiring "the old soldier," Mrs. Steady then took up a pair of canvass trowsers of a whitey-brown colour, and gradually drew them over the grey ones. These were fastened in their proper position by a large, wide strap, with its huge steel buckle in front; a coarse checked shirt, which might possibly have been once washed; and an old glazed hat, "made up" the "hero of a hundred fights"—the poor old tar who had so frequently "weathered the battle and the breeze." Mrs. Steady now produced a wooden leg, which was forthwith fixed to the supposed stump at the knee joint; finally, she added to the remaining portion of the missing arm, that red patch which we described in a former chapter.

"There!" she exclaimed, in a tone of admiration, as the last feature in that strange preparation was completed; "there, now! I should like to see the feller as can make up better nor that!"

"Ay, he'd be devilish clever, I'm thinking."

"Clever?" continued Mrs. Steady, with enthusiasm; "Vhy, there ain't a hacter in all our thehaters as could do it as vell!"

After he had finished his brandy, and presented Mrs. Steady with an extra "bob," for her private use, our actor set out to perform his various "parts."

"I must keep my veather eye open for the beaks," he murmured on entering the street.

Black Bob was a tolerable physiognomist, as will be seen by the judicious manner in which he selected his victims. He slowly proceeded along Holborn, towards the city; and, after many a scrutinising glance, at length selected from amongst the passengers an elderly lady, with a large black bonnet; it seemed to him that she could not be less than the widow of some naval officer, who had been slain in the service of his country.

Bob dragged himself towards her, rolling about like a vessel driven by the tempest.

"Good lady," mumbled he, behind her, "pray, bestow a trifle on a poor old seaman."

The lady hastened on.

"I ain't tasted anythin' the last four days!" he continued, with a pitiful accent.

Still no reply.

"Oh! kind lady," added Bob; "have compassion on a poor unfortunate sailor, who has received so many vounds that it's unpossible to vork at all, and obliges one to become a mendicant."

The lady turned round, and regarded Bob with an air of compassion.

"Have pity on a poor tar, good lady, or I shall die at yer feet vith vant."

The lady felt in her purse, and selected therefrom

---

* What are the characters to be assumed?
† Sailor, Soldier, Starved, Paralytic.

half a crown, which she compassionately placed in the extended hand of the impostor. Bob kissed the money with delight, and called down on the lady the blessings of God.

Bob hobbled onwards, glancing right and left as he went, and appealing to the passengers. He met with various degrees of success.

"Good lady!" exclaimed Bob, stopping before another victim, who, in his opinion, had the appearance of being a merchant's wife; "pray give an old sailor somethin' to keep him from dyin'."

The lady quickened her pace.

"I ain't tasted a bit for five days! Oh! have pity on a poor old tar."

The lady hastened on, but was astonished to find that the faster she proceeded, so much the more urgent became the appeals of her follower; at length, tired by the importunities of the supposed sailor, she hastily withdrew a shilling from her purse, and threw it before him. Whilst Bob was securing the gratuity, his victim escaped.

Bob became very industrious, as, in fact, he always was, when on business. He had now been out upwards of three hours, and found his receipts amounted to a tolerable sum.

"Eight and ninepence," said he to himself, whilst turning over the money in his pockets; then selecting another victim from the crowd, he obtained a further addition to his hoard.

"Pray, bestow a —" commenced Bob, once more; but, just at the moment he was about to name what he wanted, his argus eye observed the approach of a constable. He immediately started down an obscure passage, with a rapidity truly astonishing; and there was an end of the sailor.

When Bob again emerged from the gloomy retreat into which he had thus necessarily penetrated, he appeared the very picture of a weary soldier, whom service and suffering had rendered prematurely old.

Again he boldly ventured amongst the crowd, and, approaching a young lady, who appeared to be alone, commenced in his usual tone—

"Pardon, Miss, but do give a trifle to a poor old soldier, who has sarved his country thirty-five year."

It is probable that the young lady thought differently, or perchance, did not think at all about it; for she was moving away, when Master Bob placed himself before her, and somewhat more energetically repeated his demand.

"I've bin in forty-seven battles, Miss, and received seventy-eight vounds."

Finding she could not otherwise get rid of him, the young lady tendered a shilling to the mendicant.

"It is all I have left," said she, timidly.

Bob seemed to doubt that assertion, for he stood before the young girl to prevent her passing on.

"Another bob, Miss; only one shillin' more," said he in a whining tone.

"I have'nt any more, I assure you," replied the young girl, somewhat alarmed.

Bob, however, still blockaded her passage.

"I only vonts a—"

A tremendous stroke across the shoulders was at that moment lent Master Bob in lieu of the shilling which, for the third time, he was about to demand. Like a prudent man, however, Bob did not think proper to waste time in useless inquiry as to the cause of that extraordinary visitation, but at once darted off as fast as his uneven legs could carry him. He was too well acquainted with that sort of thing, and thought with the sage of old that "the better part of valour was discretion."

No sooner was our mendicant out of danger than he recommenced his piteous appeals to the sympathies of the generous. He continued thus for about two hours longer, when finding his soldier's garb not so successful as he desired, he slipped into a house of call for mendicants, and came out in a new character. His third part was that of a famishing peasant. He had thrown off his jacket, hat, and shoes; and appeared in a ragged pair of trowsers, with the shreds of an old shirt, which left the greater portion of his neck and breast quite bare. In this figure he really seemed one of the most pitiable objects that it was possible to behold.

With bare feet and uncovered head, Bob slowly crawled along the street, now directing his mute appeals to the passengers on his right and now towards the left.

Our mendicant continued this for about an hour with varied success, and was returning towards his rendezvous, when he beheld a blunt-looking member of Parliament, whom he mistook for a Sussex farmer. Bob held out his hand for a gratuity, but soon found his error in doing so; for after a moment's examination, the member raised his cane, and gratuitously dealt him half a dozen stripes across the shoulders, which were sufficient to carry the poor fellow off like a shot.

Bob now thought it time to sum up his earnings.

"Seventeen bord and a tanner,"* said he to himself; "werry fair for seven hours; but it ain't enough yet."

Master Bob made another slight change in his characteristic costume, and now appeared as a person whom paralytic limbs rendered an object of compassion and charity. He carefully selected a suitable spot on the pavement, whereon to exercise his superior talent in that "line." As soon as he

* Seventeen shillings and sixpence.

observed two or three benevolent-looking persons approaching, he gradually began those fearful twistings and convulsions which are peculiar to those afflicted with paralytic affections; in a short time a considerable crowd surrounded him, and many expressions of commiseration escaped the lips of the kind-hearted and generous.

Black Bob continued thus for upwards of an hour, and enacted the part so well, that a considerable addition to his exchequer was the result; at length, an uninvited constable poked in his nose between the bystanders, and, instead of increasing the contributions, proceeded to take our actor into custody. The latter, however, perceiving a favourable opportunity, threw his guardian down and escaped.

Our "artiste," now finding that his receipts amounted to no less than thirty-one shillings, was modest enough to consider that sufficient for a single day's work, as one of the Mendicants of London, and accordingly determined to leave off for the day.

As he was proceeding towards his residence, Bob perceived a benevolent-looking lady approaching, and found it impossible to resist the temptation for another appeal.

"That's the vidder of a good tradesman," he muttered; "I must get a bob, at least, out on her."

The lady was about to pass, when Bob, apparently by accident, reeled before her.

"Pardon, good Missus."

"Don't mention it, my good master," returned the lady, who was about to proceed on her way.

"Pray bestow a trifle on a poor creeter, who has broken his leg and lost his arm."

Bob received no response; he, however, was not to be so easily put off.

"Pray, good Missus," he continued, in a sepulchral tone, still following at her side; "I ain't a penny to buy a crust vith."

Still no reply.

"Pray, Missus, have pity on a starvin' creeter; I ain't —"

In the midst of his pitiful appeal, Bob felt the pressure of a heavy hand fall on his shoulders; he did not take the trouble to turn, with the view to ascertain who it was, for he correctly imagined that such a blow could come from none other than a constable of muscular strength.

By a movement, rapid as lightning, he stooped down, twisted out of his enemy's grasp, and before the latter had time to assume a defensive attitude Bob's left fist fell upon his stomach, with a force which re-echoed like the sound of a drum. That blow sent the constable sprawling in the mud, to the infinite delight of the bystanders; and Bob

again escaped. He was very well satisfied with his day's performances, and, as the evening was getting far advanced, hastened his steps towards St. Giles's.

"That'll do for vonce," said he, proceeding leisurely down Snow-hill; I thought it looked fine veather for beggin'."

In passing down that declivity, Bob's attentive eye caught sight of a great crowd assembled at its base. In the centre of that throng, two carriages appeared to have accidentally come in contact, and thereby almost destroyed. Four or five horses, of superior breed and condition, were plunging and kicking in the midst of the crowd.

Bob's eye winked, his ears tingled, and his fingers itched, as he beheld that sight; he hurried towards the scene of confusion, with the delight of one who anticipates a rich treat.

He had penetrated into the thickest part of the crowd just at the moment when an elderly lady was being carried from one of the carriages, in a state of insensibility. That lady wore a superb gold watch, and was accompanied by a pale young man, equally well furnished with the records of time.

Now Master Robert Bantam, otherwise Bob the bruiser, alias Black Bob—was an "artist" in more respects than one. We have already seen how successful he had been as a mendicant; as a dealer in the curiosities of female loveliness; and as the conductor of dark plots, having private assassination for their object: we have now to behold his ability in the delicate art of "subtraction."

Rushing upon the lady and young man (who appeared to be her son), as if driven by the crowd, Bob ingeniously contrived to bring the little group to the ground, and while in that position, skilfully transferred two watches from the persons of those who had previously possessed them, to the better security of his own pockets.

He now hastened to extricate himself from the group; and in five minutes afterwards might have been observed stealing up Field-lane, towards a dirty looking shop, which exhibited in its dark body articles of every imaginable description.

After hastily glancing around, Bob walked into the shop. A little girl, who sat upon an old stool, appeared to be the only person on the premises.

"Is old Ben in?" inquired Master Bantam.

"Ees, he is."

"I vants to see him."

The little girl raised a small square piece of the flooring, which seemed to answer the purpose of a trap door, and called out as loudly as her weak shrill voice would permit,

"Here's somebody wants ye."

A low mumbling noise was heard approaching

the aperture, and presently the bald head of an old man arose from beneath. His long features, slightly angular, and large protruding nose, denoted a true member of the Jewish persuasion.

"Who ish it as vonts me?" inquired the head.

"Oh! come up Ben; ye knows I don't come 'xcept on bisniss," replied Bob.

"Ah!" exclaimed the old man with a smile, as he screwed himself through the aperture, "Ish't you, my tear! Vell vots up?"

"I's two spank logs (gold watches) to svop," responded Bob, pulling out the watches he had recently stolen.

It is unnecessary to detail the particulars of the conversation wherein a bargain was struck for the sale of those watches; sufficient to say that Bob obtained twenty guineas for them; which, as near as he could guess, was nearly one-fourth their value.

Once more our artiste directed his steps towards St. Giles's, where, after sundry trifling stoppages on the way, he at length arrived as the parish clock was striking eight.

He found Mrs. Steady comfortably seated before a roaring fire, with a bottle of her favourite liquor by her side, and in that state which sailors term "three sheets in the wind;" but which we should consider at least seven, or seven sheets and a remnant.

—o—

CHAPTER XIV.

"APPROACHING EVENTS CAST THEIR SHADOWS BEFORE THEM."

AFTER Black Bob had seated himself by the side of his beloved "five foot six," and turned his attention to that worthy creature, he beheld a singular and extraordinary change in her manner, for which he was unable to account. That Mrs. Steady had been indulging in her favourite liquor, was nothing new; neither would it appear strange had she been incapable of moving. On the present occasion, however, she moved too fast—in fact could not sit still. She turned round on her seat incessantly, and her head, hands, and legs were in perpetual motion.

"Vot's the matter vith ye?" inquired Bob.

Instead, however, of replying to the question, Mrs. Steady, evidently becoming more agitated, turned towards the bottle by her side, probably to see if it would answer for her. She poured out a hornful, but in doing so her hand shook so dreadfully that Bob could not avoid noticing it, and his suspicions were much excited thereby.

"Vot is the matter?" demanded Bob, peremptorily.

"Nothin' pertickler," muttered Mrs. Steady between her closed teeth, as she vainly endeavoured to convey the liquor to her lips without wasting it.

"I knows better," rejoined Bob in a loud voice; "and I'm d—d if"——

"Vot?" interrupted his wife in a firm tone, after taking a draught of her favourite spirit.

"I tell ye there's summut wrong," replied Bob, "and by G— I'll know vot it is, or"——

"Vell, here's luck," interrupted Steady, with returning confidence, as she tossed off the liquor remaining in the horn.

Bob fancied he might be mistaken; that the tremulousness of his amiable partner was the result of the latter having drank something which had disagreed with her: it was very probable, certainly.

"She ain't drunk," mused Bob, "seein' as how she can sit upright; though I thinks hers three or four sheets in the vind, as the sayin' is."

The worthy object of these remarks placed her elbows on the table, and dropped her head between her hands for the purpose of taking a short nap.

The amiable couple were consequently silent for several minutes.

"I aint satisfied, not by no means," murmured Bob, restlessly. "If so be as she's "——

Master Bantam abruptly interrupted himself, cast an anxious glance towards his treasure, and another on his "fine" wife. The latter appeared to be dozing comfortably; nevertheless one could distinctly perceive an unusual paleness on that portion of those rough features which were visible to the eye.

Bob was sorely perplexed. He, however, resolved to ascertain at once if his suspicions were correct, and accordingly went towards the chest wherein his costumes were deposited, under pretence of looking for a useful article, but in reality for the purpose of seeing if any were missing.

The moment his back was turned towards Mrs. Steady, that loving lady stealthily drew a small, mysterious packet from her bosom, and emptied its contents into the horn. She then poured out a quantity of spirits from the bottle before her and pretended to drink.

"Thee'st had too much of that a'ready," observed Bob on leaving the chest with a satisfied air.

"May be I has," rejoined his wife in a surly voice; "howsomever I vonts more on it. Hav'nt ye got a bob or two for some?"

Now Bob wished to get rid of his wife's presence, in order that he might examine his hoard, and accordingly replied—

"Here you are, old voman; there's a bob for some grog, and two more for grub, cause I'm get-in' confounded hungry. Lets ha' some of Mother Maud's sauserges."

Mrs. Steady received the money without observation, and hastened into the street as she was. Bob silently followed her to the door, which he fastened as before, and then returned to his apartment. After having lighted his lamp, he proceeded at once towards his treasure, which he examined with more than ordinary attention and solicitude. Unable however to detect any diminution therein, as it stood, he carefully arranged it in a particular form, and added thereto the amount which he had received during the day. That done, he once more closed the aperture, and returned to his seat.

For upwards of a quarter of an hour he continued in a musing attitude before the fire.

" I'm blowed if I can make it out, at all!" he muttered; " she's as white as a sheet, and trembles as if her had been stiffin' (murdering) a body."

As he raised himself into a perpendicular position his eye caught sight of the bottle with the horn by its side. Feeling thirsty as well as hungry our artiste naturally raised the horn to his lips and drained it at a draught. After this he sat for nearly half an hour awaiting the return of his lovely partner.

" I wish Steady would come; for I'm gettin' confounded hungry."

He waited another half hour, but still no one came; then, finding himself getting ill, went and stretched himself on his bed, where, for the present we will leave him, in order to watch the proceedings of his " loving wife" Steady.

On entering the open street, the latter slowly proceeded towards the dirty tavern which we have before seen her visit. She called for a glass of gin, and instead of paying for it with the money Bob had given her, tendered a bright guinea in exchange. The landlady took it as a matter of course, and gave the worthy customer the change with a smile significantly expressive.

" Bob's money, eh?" she whispered.

" All right!" replied Steady in a similar tone.

The latter drank off the liquor she had thus purchased, and giving a familiar nod to the landlady, once more issued into the open air.

" 'In two hours arter it's took, he'll be a corpus,' ses the old pisoner. I vonder if he's took it," murmured Steady, as she walked towards an old house in Field-lane whither she had frequently retreated when circumstances became serious.*

The mysterious and obscure building towards

* The Old House in Field-lane was pulled down in 1847, by the City Improvement Commissioners. It created a great sensation at the time.

which Mrs. Steady now directed her steps, was long celebrated among thieves and murderers as a place of secure retreat. Here she remained during the greater part of the night. About four o'clock in the morning, however, she sent a faithful emissary to reconnoitre her residence. After an absence of two hours, the latter returned in a state of great excitement.

" Vot's the news?" enquired Steady, eagerly.

" There's a devil of a doo, and everybody was axin arter you."

" And vot did ye say?"

" I said as how I seed ye lyin' dead drunk as usual, and shoved ye up a passage."

" Vell?"

" Then Bill Bull and Weasel (who had been arter Bob), axed me vhere it was. So I takes 'em to a out-o'-the-way place, and said it vos there. But in course somebody had carried yer off!"

" Bull and Weasel, did ye say?" enquired Steady with a diabolical grin.

" Ay, and Stringer too."

" Good!" muttered Steady delighted; " I has it!"

A fiendish idea had at that moment entered the brain of the besotted Steady, who immediately proceeded to arrange her plans for carrying it out.

Aware that her husband must have been poisoned by the deleterious powder which she herself had surreptitiously placed before him, it seemed to strike her that she could not better ward off suspicion from herself, than by accusing Bull, Weasel, and Stringer with the murder.

" That's a good idear," she muttered; " and I'll carry it out at vonce."

Accordingly Mrs. Steady arose, tied a coarse handkerchief round her head, arranged her dress to appear as if she had just carelessly rose from her drunken couch, and proceeded towards her abode, which she entered as if still incapable of walking steady.

An old woman was found sitting with a neighbour in charge of the apartments, and around the door were several groups assembled in earnest conversation. The latter made way for Mrs. Steady on her approach, and offered their sympathy and condolence.

" Vot's the matter? Who's done it?" she inquired in a faltering tone.

The two women hastened to explain all they knew, and in conclusion observed, " that the thing looked very black."

" Werry black," repeated Mrs. Steady, affecting a lamentable tone; " but I al'ys thought that Bill Bull and his pals"——

" Does ye surspict Bill then?" interrupted the woman who lived next door.

"In coarse!" replied the other, in order, perhaps, to protect "the poor widdy" in her embarrassing position; "don't ye rec'lect him and his pals' vos found here? Aint it nat'ral to surspect 'em?"

"Vell I'm sure," added the former in a tone of surprise, but without deigning to state on what precise point she was so well satisfied.

It is, perhaps, unnecessary that we should describe, minutely, the details of what followed. Suffice it to say that the wretched creature followed out her diabolical scheme to the letter, and the result was the trial and execution of Bill Bull, Weasel and Stringer.

When she had accomplished this masterpiece of iniquity, Mrs. Steady took time to consider how she should proceed; for which purpose she became a voluntary prisoner in her own hovel, and only ventured out at night to replenish her cupboard and gin bottles.

On the night after the execution of her victims, Mrs. Steady determined to ascertain the exact extent of that hoarding, which was the real cause of all her guilt, adopting the same precautions as her first victim and wretched husband had twice before effected. She then paid another visit to her gin bottle, picked up the lamp and approached the hole where Bob had deposited his hoardings. After several ineffectual efforts, she at length touched the spring, and the whole treasure was exposed to view. She picked up several pieces, and examined them with peculiar delight. When fully satisfied with the appearance of the precious metal, Mrs. Steady carefully spread out on the floor a well worn, but clean sheet, and commenced arranging the treasure there n. This occupied her, with little pauses of admiration and reflection, the greater part of three hours; at the end of which, she found there had been no less than three thousand one hundred and eighty six guineas deposited in the hole.

"Oh! ye beauties!" she exclaimed, surveying the glittering treasure, as its shining heaps stood in fascinating rank and file; "ye shall go into the country, as Bob"—

The guilty woman interrupted herself, as that name passed her lips. A nervous trembling added to the effects of increasing intoxication, lent her features a lowering and hideous appearance.

"I must shake this off," she muttered, once more attacking the gin bottle; "it vont do to be a coward now. The job's done, and there's an end on it."

The wind ominously resounded through the filthy passages of the building, and seemed to give a moaning negative to Mrs. Steady's soliloquy.

"No!" she exclaimed, in the utmost alarm; "who says no?"

The guilty wretch listened attentively for several minutes, but not hearing a repetition of the imaginary voice, sat down with the view to calm her excited feelings.

The effects of the liquor which she had drunk, added to other exertions, all combined to render her extremely somnolent; she therefore laid her head upon the table, and remained in that position for upwards of half an hour.

The sleep of great criminals is but seldom sound or refreshing, and that of Mrs. Steady formed no exception to the general rule. At the expiration of the half hour alluded to, she suddenly arose, and with eyes dilated to the utmost extremity, glanced towards the chest of her murdered husband.

"Vot do ye vant?" she exclaimed, frightfully alarmed. "I didn't do it! It vos yerself as took it, Bob me darlin'."

Then turning round towards the door, the wretched creature gazed with outstretched eyes and trembling limbs, as if some new attack was meditated on her.

"Out vith ye!" she exclaimed; "out vith ye all three!"

As the imaginary figures appeared to depart, Mrs. Steady once more sank down upon her seat—but not to rest, although she was quite exhausted. In a few minutes she again raised her head, and glanced around the room with an air of wildness that already indicated approaching derangement.

"Ah! ah! ah!" she at length chuckled hysterically. "Gone, be ye! Ah! good luck to ye!"

Mrs. Steady thereupon bounded towards the heaps of gold with which she had recently so much amused herself, and, hastily taking up several pieces, threw them after the imaginary intruders. Then she began to dance round her hoard, and presently fell down upon the heap quite exhausted.

There she lay with the lamp still burning upon the table, and the cast iron stove still roaring with heat.

Two hours had thus passed; the lamp flickering, and the fire blazing; when the wind, which blew keenly out of doors, added its low moaning to the obscurity of that scene. By and by the air gaining strength with the outward hurricane, penetrated those foul passages, and found vent in small gusts through the keyhole of the door. Apparently bent on mischief, it played round the stove, in the corners of the apartment, between the legs of the table, and, finally approached the lamp. In a moment, the falling wick was thus conveyed to some combustible material about the person of the sleeping maniac, who, half an hour afterwards, perished in the flames which destroyed all.

—o—

CHAPTER XV.

"ALL THINGS MUST HAVE AN END."
AND so must our brief " eventful history."

After the conclusion of the ball at Littlemore House, Harry Vernon retraced his steps towards his residence.

We have already described the short pungent conversation between him and our hero, as also the prospective result thereof. It therefore only remains for us to record as briefly as possible the details of what followed that energetic meeting.

The moment Harry Vernon entered his library he opened his desk, arranged the materials for writing, and hastily penned the following billets :—

"6, Grafton-street, Thursday midnight.
"Dear Dawson,

"I saw that demon Duro this evening, at Lord Littlemore's ball. You will guess the result. I meet him to-morrow morning by break of day at Chalk Farm, and shall be obliged to you to accompany me thither.　　Believe me,
　　In great haste, yours truly,
　　　　HARRY VERNON."

The other, which was addressed to his brother, ran thus :—

"Dear Victor,

"If you can make it convenient to return with the bearer, I shall be exceedingly gratified, as I am anxious to confer with you on a subject of paramount—nay, vital importance.
　　　　"Yours,
　　　　　"HARRY."

Dr. Dawson received his missive with becoming gravity. As long as those brutal laws, which allowed one man to destroy another in cold blood, still disgraced the statute book, he felt that there was no alternative for a duel, if, indeed, it were desirable to avoid one. The worthy physician, however, seemed desirous of taking the quarrel upon himself, or, at all events, of sharing it with his early friend, Harry Vernon.

"Tell your master," said he to the servant who brought him Harry's note, "that I will do myself the pleasure of waiting upon him in half-an-hour."

When the physician arrived in Grafton street, he found Harry Vernon busily engaged in the melancholy operation of " setting his house in order," by way of anticipating the worst.

"Never say die," observed Dawson upon hearing the object of those wise precautions; "though I must admit that he appears to be matchless with his weapons."

"No matter, my dear friend," replied Harry;

"it is at all events as well to be prepared, for I am determined that one of us shall die !"

"Yes!" added Dr. Dawson abstractedly; "it is necessary he should die; and if you do not kill him, I will !"

"You!" exclaimed Harry with surprise.

"Yes! That is, if he be not proof against steel or lead."

"But why, my friend ?"

"Because he has seriously injured me."

"Indeed! I thought no one suffered like myself."

"Alas! That man is a wholesale brigand and murderer."

"I thought so too," murmured Harry; "and yet it seems incredible to me that "——-

"Nothing is too black for that villain, believe me," interrupted Dawson.

"Why, my friend, how has he injured you ?"

"He is my rival!"

"Yours ? "

"Yes! he has stolen the affection of my cousin! You and I are, therefore, brothers in misfortune."

Harry Vernon instantly arose, and, taking the hand of Dr. Dawson, shook it warmly.

"We will punish him, brother," said he, as a commiserating tear glided down his cheek and fell on the physician's hand.

At an early hour on the following morning, while yet the dusky hue of night lingered on the horizon, a single coach was observed driving rapidly towards the Chalk Farm meadows. On its stopping at the foot of the hill, three gentlemen, enveloped in cloaks, and disguised with masks, descended; the first carried a case of suspicious form; the second was provided with a sort of bag or long package; and the other stayed behind for a moment in order to give some directions to the coachman.

All three passed round towards the western base of the hill, and there awaited the arrival of others.

In about a quarter of an hour, another carriage was heard approaching; it drew up at some distance from the first, yet just within sight, and three gentlemen, similarly attired to those who had first arrived, at once alighted, and directed their steps to the spot where the others stood awaiting them.

One of each party then stepped aside, and after apparently consulting for a few moments, returned, and, producing a pair of swords, presented one to each of the two members of that mysterious group. The latter then threw off their cloaks and masks, and placed themselves in position for the deadly strife.

The two gentlemen who thus approached each other with that hostile bearing, were, as our readers will doubtless suppose, the celebrated Duke de

Duro and Harry Vernon. Each appeared quite cool and collected; but a dark frown overspread the countenance of the former, whilst that of the latter seemed pale and careworn.

After several passes without any serious effect, Harry, becoming impatient, made a vigorous lunge, which was admirably parried by his antagonist, who, in his turn, with better skill, sent his weapon completely through the body of poor Harry. Though mortally wounded, the latter declared his wish to renew the combat, but Dr. Dawson whispered a few words in his ear, and after giving some directions about attending to the wound, Harry was removed to a short distance.

Another consultation then took place, at the termination of which one of those engaged in it proceeded to measure the ground, whilst the other opened the mysterious case, and took therefrom a brace of pistols.

"That's too much," observed Dr. Dawson, as the gentleman was stepping along; "twelve paces, you know."

"Six, if you like, my dear sir," added de Duro, with the utmost *sang froid.*

"Be it so, then," rejoined the physician coldly.

A further consultation was thereupon held between the seconds, who afterwards acceded to the arrangement, and then retired to a short distance.

The Duke de Duro seemed astonished by the cool manner in which his own proposition had been accepted by his new opponent. He accordingly felt just cause for alarm, and eyed the physician with one of those annihilating glances which had so often struck terror into the hearts of his enemies. Dr. Dawson, however, was now proof against such an attack, and regarded his antagonist with a steady eye. He had other grounds for seeking "satisfaction" than those of mere rivalry, and recollected with perfect indifference the boasting assertion of his opponent, who "*never left an enemy alive!*"

"Now, (thought he,) we are upon pretty equal terms; and if killed myself, you shall fall too!"

The combatants regarded each other with wrathful earnestness, and prepared to take the advantage of a first fire. So intent upon this point were they, that the instant the signal was given both shots resounded as though but one had fired. Both, too, had aimed with deadly effect, for at the moment that the ball of De Duro entered the breast of Dr. Dawson, that of the latter penetrated between the eye-lashes of his antagonist, and each fell to the ground at the same time. The Duke never spoke afterwards, but Dr. Dawson had just sufficient strength left to raise his hand towards his expiring friend Harry Vernon, in token of his costly triumph.

CHAPTER XVI.

THE BEGINNING OF THE END.

About three months after the events related in the preceding chapter, important meetings were simultaneously held at the Three Topers, the Jolly Beggars, and several other houses of noted resort for the Mendicants of London. It seemed that some grave and momentous subject occupied the minds of all who were thus brought together, for none but persons of full age, and undoubted members of the fraternity, were permitted to join those assemblages.

The meeting which assembled at the Jolly Beggars appeared the most important of all, and hourly received reports from each of the other gatherings. At midnight a bell resounded through the passages of the house, and the next moment, all those assembled in the various apartments of the tavern were observed to proceed along a secret avenue; thence down an extensive flight of steps; and finally enter a spacious room, bearing some resemblance to a chapel.

The first thing that took place after all had entered, was the appearance of certain members on a raised platform. One of the oldest of these was then called upon to preside over the meeting. The latter at once proceeded to address his brethren in a feeling and judicious speech. He said they were assembled for the double purpose of rendering all homage to the memory of their late King, and also to elect a fit and proper person to succeed him. He dilated in glowing terms on the distinguished merit, and brilliant career of Andrew Armstrong, who by his superb talents, had raised himself from the humble condition of a sickly gipsy boy, to be a grandee of Spain, of France, and, more than all, King of the Mendicants of England.

Hymns were then sung, and other formalities gone through; after which the meeting proceeded to the election of a new King of the Mendicants.

Similar proceedings took place at each of the other assemblages; and, afterwards, a box containing the voting papers was carefully conveyed to the central meeting. When those papers had been duly examined, and the votes cast up, it turned out that Blind Bolton, otherwise Sir Samuel Seelie, alias le Comte de Carvaez, was the successful candidate; and arrangements were then commenced for his early coronation.

Among the Mendicants of London matters went on much as usual, under the new reign (a narrative of which we may, on some future occasion, have the pleasure of presenting to the notice of our readers); but at the west end, and in the brilliant reunions of Paris and Madrid, the Duke de Duro's loss was felt as a national calamity.

The Duchess of Durillo gradually became more irritative as old age crept on, and she finally resolved to retire to her native scenes about Seville; but before doing so, however, she expressed an earnest wish to see her adopted daughter appropriately settled in life, according to the promises she had at first made to her.

Thus, after some negociation, the desired object was attained, and the news went forth that the Viscount Victor Vernon was about to marry Her Highness the Princess Mary of Seville.

Another union, though by no means of equal importance to that we have just recorded, took place about the same time, but at the other extremity of the metropolis. Captain Cable at length began to fancy he saw extraordinary charms in the plump and rosy features of the merry hostess (whose tavern monopolised so much of the jovial officer's time), which perfections had hitherto escaped his penetrating eye. How it was, he could not for the life of him conceive; nevertheless, Captain Cable became incontrovertibly convinced of the fact. He consequently proposed, was accepted, and eventually became the popular landlord of the Thames Tap.

When the result of the fatal duel reached the ears of Lady Longton and Miss Littlemore, both were sensibly affected, especially the latter, who gradually declined in health, and in six months afterwards was said to have died of a broken heart.

The firm of Armstrong and Co. experienced a sad loss in the death of its leading member. Nevertheless Messieurs Johnson, Mole, and Rolt, together with the beautiful Mrs. Thompson, continued to do business as if nothing unusual or extraordinary had occurred. Indeed, if anything, they seemed more industrious than ever. The little coteries which assembled at the Pot and Pipe, and other places of similar resort, still held occasional consultations on the subject, but as nothing transpired to throw light on the proceedings of the past, these worthies were ultimately obliged to abandon all further inquiry from perfect inanition.

Mrs. Brown, Mrs. Green, and Mrs. Blue, would sometimes meet, and, over a cup of their favourite beverage, discuss the events of the past. At times, too, they would solemnly enter into lengthened speculations on the future, and the probable changes that might occur in the mysterious affairs of that strange establishment.

The death of Black Bob convinced Mr. Ledger that he had lost the thirty guineas which he had paid that worthy. He also knew perfectly well that without the assistance of such an accomplished cut-throat he would himself be unable to secure the object which, under present circumstances, was so necessary for his own interest. Finding it impossible to proceed any further in the matter, and seeing that the Marquis of Minchington was determined to ascertain the state of his affairs, the dishonest steward committed suicide to avoid the consequences of his evil conduct.

Of the other characters in our "eventful history," three or four only remain that call for especial notice ere we conclude.

The moody Mr. Muffle, after enduring for some time the remorse which his revengeful crime had inflicted on him, at length became an inmate of a lunatic asylum. His affectionate and suffering sister, whom we first introduced to the notice of our readers, by incessant labour as sempstress at length worked an early passage to her grave.

In the course of a few years that dumpling of a mendicant, the facetious Master Timbers, followed the example of "all flesh," and, like others, was carried to that place "from whence no traveller returns."

Mr. Scrieve on the contrary, became more vigorous than ever, and shortly after the removal of his friend Muffle concocted a new scheme for robbing the public. Instead of begging for assistance, he now wrote to inform his readers that for a trifling consideration, he would tell them "something to their advantage;" and upon receiving the desired recompence, advised all his correspondents to BE. WARE OF

THE MENDICANTS OF LONDON!

THE END.

J. STEWARD, PRINTER, 1, HARFORD-PLACE, DRURY LANE.

www.ingramcontent.com/pod-product-compliance
Lightning Source LLC
Chambersburg PA
CBHW081213170626
46811CB00010B/3277